APACHE

He didn't dare make a move until he learned where they were. A fly or two buzzed by him and some quail whistled nearby. No Apaches. Some doves cooed and then flapped their wings as they left a nearby juniper.

Was that a sign? Through the sights on his rifle, he studied the thick evergreen boughs for any sign. He dried his left hand on his pants. The bitter smell of spent gunpowder in his nostrils, he listened hard.

Then a buck burst out of the boughs that Slocum was staring hard at, brandishing a cap-and-ball pistol aimed at him. He looked down the sights and fired. Behind him a war cry cut the air as another Apache bore down on him with a tomahawk. Slocum was bringing the rifle around. Another shot rang out, and the racing Indian jerked his head up and broke his stride as a second bullet struck him in the back.

On his feet, Slocum was ready to bust him with his own rifle, when the buck wilted into a pile before him. Riding down the bench through the junipers with a smoking pistol in his fist was his scout Chewy.

Slocum dropped his chin and shook his head—too damn close.

JAKE LOGAN

SLOCUM
AND THE
APACHE CAMPAIGN

J

JOVE BOOKS, NEW YORK

THE BERKLEY PUBLISHING GROUP
Published by the Penguin Group
Penguin Group (USA) Inc.
375 Hudson Street, New York, New York 10014, USA
Penguin Group (Canada), 90 Eglinton Avenue East, Suite 700, Toronto, Ontario M4P 2Y3, Canada
(a division of Pearson Penguin Canada Inc.)
Penguin Books Ltd., 80 Strand, London WC2R 0RL, England
Penguin Group Ireland, 25 St. Stephen's Green, Dublin 2, Ireland (a division of Penguin Books Ltd.)
Penguin Group (Australia), 250 Camberwell Road, Camberwell, Victoria 3124, Australia
(a division of Pearson Australia Group Pty. Ltd.)
Penguin Books India Pvt. Ltd., 11 Community Centre, Panchsheel Park, New Delhi—110 017, India
Penguin Group (NZ), 67 Apollo Drive, Mairangi Bay, Auckland 1311, New Zealand
(a division of Pearson New Zealand Ltd.)
Penguin Books (South Africa) (Pty.) Ltd., 24 Sturdee Avenue, Rosebank, Johannesburg 2196,
South Africa

Penguin Books Ltd., Registered Offices: 80 Strand, London WC2R 0RL, England

This is a work of fiction. Names, characters, places, and incidents either are the product of the author's imagination or are used fictitiously, and any resemblance to actual persons, living or dead, business establishments, events, or locales is entirely coincidental.

SLOCUM AND THE APACHE CAMPAIGN

A Jove Book / published by arrangement with the author

PRINTING HISTORY
Jove edition / May 2007

ISBN: 978-0-515-14299-0

JOVE®
Jove Books are published by The Berkley Publishing Group,
a division of Penguin Group (USA) Inc.,
375 Hudson Street, New York, New York 10014.
JOVE is a registered trademark of Penguin Group (USA) Inc.
The "J" design is a trademark belonging to Penguin Group (USA) Inc.

PRINTED IN THE UNITED STATES OF AMERICA

10 9 8 7 6 5 4 3 2 1

PROLOGUE

Heat waves distorted the faraway mountains. Mary Jennifer Harbor blinked her dry blue eyes at the hazy peaks from under the brim of Jed Slade's sweat-stinking felt hat. No matter about the distant ranges—how far away was water? Her dry mouth and throat reminded her the only liquid she had managed to locate in the past twenty-four hours was from a barrel cactus she'd found under the lacy shade of a mesquite tree. With a sharp rock she'd finally busted into the spiny bundle and took several pieces of the watermelon-like flesh to chew on as quick as she could. It had not been sweet or cool or good tasting, but it had been wet. There weren't even any of them in the country she stumbled through that morning.

Nineteen, unmarried, she'd came to Arizona to teach school. What would her finishing school friends in St. Louis think of her now? Poor Mary—lost in an endless desert—her very best dress ripped and torn, the hem in dusty rags and the bustle wearing sores on her hip. Indecent or not, in the darkness of the night before, she'd undressed, shed her confining corset and cast it aside—too hot and too binding for her to move in. The bustle was next. She'd have done that already, but she knew she'd have to stop and rip the dress's length shorter if she abandoned the bustle, or the trailing parts would hang on every stickery bush in this *damned* prickly country.

Her language, she noticed, had turned to be like the vocab-

ulary of the driver Jed Slade who'd driven her in the buckboard from Lordsburg. The regular stage had been wrecked,
the driver killed, so Slade agreed to haul her and the mail in a
buckboard to Bowie, Arizona. He had mentioned, between
spitting tobacco to the side and wiping his whisker-bristled
mouth on the back of his unwashed hands, that the barrel cactus was edible and a water source. Pointed them out to her in
passing. He'd said a lot more about the desert and survival.
She wished she'd listened closer, but his revolting unwashed
body odor kept filling her nose, and sitting with her hip and
shoulder touching him on the spring seat made her skin crawl.

When he claimed the streak of smoke in the sky was from
Indians attacking the next stage stop—her heart quit.

"We've got to get off this gawdamn road. Them red fuckers
will be swarming on us like ants before you know it." He turned
the team south and headed off through the flat desert at breakneck speed, dodging bushes as he was about to upset them. Her
right hand grasped the iron side rail and the other the board seat
under her for dear life. She kept breathing in deep. For her to
faint would surely mean her death falling off the jolting hell-
bent wagon.

"Damn you sonsabitches!" Slade swore at the racing horses
as he stood up to turn them in time before they struck a ditch.

"Mr. Slade, is this necessary?" she finally managed to get out.

"Hell, you bet your pretty ass it is!" He shook his head in
disgusted disbelief, as if he could not imagine she would even
ask such a thing. "Why, them red devils would bust your cherry
faster then you can say Simon Brown."

"What do you mean?" She fought down her dress after they
bounced over another bump.

"Why, they'd rape you, girl. Them red niggers would stick
their dicks in you like a porcupine shoots quills in a dog's
nose."

She felt her face turn crimson red. He was talking about
things she kept out of her mind—acts she didn't even imagine
because they were so horrible. So gross, nice girls never even
whispered them to true friends. Here she was in the middle of
nowhere with the most vulgar man she could ever imagine lived

on the face of the earth, on a wild ride to hell. The New Mexico-Arizona Stage line management would certainly get a very sharp letter from her about his obscene behavior when this was all over.

He wheeled the lathered, hard-breathing horses into a dry wash and stood up to stop them. "Whoa! Sorry, there ain't no facilities here. But it's better to be alive to piss here than dead and doing it in the hereafter."

Her face heated again with embarrassment and she quicklike glanced aside.

"Don't wander fur. We're smack-dab in the heart of Apache country." He got off, unbuttoned his pants, and she looked away in time not to see what he had extracted.

But facing the north, she could hear the stream of his urination. What an animal. How could she ever get clear of him? How far away was Bowie? At the base of some mountains? He must have really had to go, for she could still hear it running.

"That's better," he said and she dared not to look.

"Aw, you probably never seen a pecker big as mine before," he said, getting back on the seat beside her.

"I am not interested in your anatomy. Let's get on to Bowie." She gave him all the room on the seat she could. He was still too close to her.

"Damn, I never knowed that was what they called it. It's an *an—at—tommy*. By Gawd, I heard 'em called dicks, pricks and dongs on a donkey, but not that. Course I ain't educated like you are."

She sat up straight and squared her shoulders. "Can we go now?"

He spat aside, then nodded at the team. "We ain't got no fresh horses to change here—got to let these cool a spell."

"Walk them then."

"Listen, darling." His fetid breath in her face and his possessive arm hugging her shoulder, he moved against her. "What you need is a little loving."

"Get your hands off me this minute."

"I like a gal's got spunk. I've had 'em tried to buck me off before, but by grab, I kept my old pecker stuck in their cunt till the end. Bet you'd buck some too." He pulled her around to face him, his yellow teeth exposed and his beady eyes boring holes in her like a wild animal. In the struggle to defend herself, she felt his hand try to squeeze her breast through the corset. She caught her breath in cold fear at the thought of him fondling her.

In a fit of Herculean pent-up rage, she rose and shoved him off the wagon seat. She was still in his iron grasp, and they both went flying onto the ground in a pile. At their screams, the spooked team bolted and tore out. She looked in fear at the unmoving Slade pinned underneath her, then glanced in shock at the departing horses and buckboard. They were running away at breakneck speed. At last she rose to her knees, and realized as the numbness began to evaporate that he no longer held her in his grasp. Knelt beside him on the ground and short of breath, she rubbed her sore arms and noticed that his eyes were wide open, but not blinking.

"Slade—Slade, the damn horses have ran off." She slapped him hard. "Wake up, stupid!"

Nothing.

She peered at the darkening pool of blood on the ground beneath his head. His stark white forehead was exposed since he'd lost his weather-beaten felt hat in the spill. The thin gray black hair ruffled in the hot desert wind—nearly bald. His whiskered jaw was slack, the half-rotten, yellow lower teeth and brown tobacco wad exposed. Must have hit a sharp rock on the back of his head in the fall. She pushed herself off of him—then his leg gave a final involuntary kick and she screamed. Then fainted.

1

With his jackknife, he cut little curls of wood off the small block of juniper in his palm. Squatted under a mesquite tree, he waited in the afternoon heat. No need to be in any hurry. At her present course she'd waltz right past him on the game trail. He'd seen her coming that direction almost thirty minutes earlier through his brass telescope from off the ridge. A nice-looking young white woman in a one-time expensive dress, a little tattered and dusty, and certainly not where she belonged—there would be a story there.

She was deep in Apache country. Not the ideal place for an attractive tenderfoot woman to wander around in with no canteen or horse. He rubbed his callused index finger over his sun-cracked lip. Had to be an interesting explanation in this, and she'd soon be where he squatted. He could hear her hard breathing and the sounds of her shoe soles on the gravelly ground.

"Oh," she groaned and looked around as she came off the rise toward his site.

He busied himself notching the juniper until she was almost past him. Then he glanced up at her tattered, dusty hem and smiled. "You looking for a streetcar?"

At the sound of his voice, she shrieked and whirled. "Who—who're you?"

He looked up from his carving, knowing that eye contact

with a flighty horse or an upset person sometimes panicked them. "You must be lost."

"I am. Who're you?"

He kept his attention on the block and his knife. "They call me Slocum."

"What—what're you doing out here?"

He looked up, closing down his left eye. "I live out here. What's your excuse?"

"Oh . . ." Her mud-streaked handsome face looked too red from exertion and the sun. The blue eyes tried to read something about him.

"I never heard your name, ma'am." He rose and removed his dented four-corner hat with the stiff brim and trailing chin string.

"Ah—Mary—Mary Harbor. I'm going to Bowie. They're expecting me." She swallowed, then wet her cracked lips and swallowed again before she managed to square her shoulders. "I'm going to teach school there."

"How did you get out here?" Out of habit, he shifted the .44 in his holster.

She threw her arm back to the east and looked pained. "He said Indians were attacking the stage station and we had to go across country."

"He?"

"Yes, he—Jed Slade. The man driving the rig."

"And?"

"Well, he drove like crazy out through the desert for miles and then he said the horses needed a rest." Her eyes squeezed shut and tears spilled down her cheeks. "And then he attacked me."

He folded up his jackknife and pocketed it. "Attack you?"

She nodded swiftly. "And I tried to escape him. We fell out of the wagon struggling and the horses ran away. Jed—Mr. Slade hit his head on a rock. He died."

"When was that?"

"Two days ago. I think."

"I have a canteen on my horse. I imagine you need a drink." He started for the hipshot roan horse behind the short trees.

"Oh, yes. How did you find me?"

"I guess, Miss Harbor, you found me." He lifted the canteen and handed it to her.

She made a face and looked around as if to locate something to tie him there. "You live out here?"

"Mostly."

She screamed in horror, and he whipped around to frown, then laugh at her fear-filled look. "He won't hurt you. That's Chako. He's an Apache scout."

She held the canteen he gave her in both hands and trembled.

"It'll be all right." Slocum tried to assure her.

Her eyes turned blank, knees buckled, and he moved in to sweep her up in his arms.

"Go get my bedroll." He tossed his head at the teenage Apache with his red headband, a faded army shirt, breechcloth, and knee-high, pointed toed moccasins.

Chako smiled. "Guess I look plenty bad."

"No, she's been through hell to get here. You seen a team and buggy?"

"No, why?" Chako asked, undoing Slocum's roll from the saddle and bringing it over. He unfurled it.

"She and Jed Slade were coming this way, I take it, and they thought—he anyway thought Indians were attacking a stage station, so he took off into the desert."

"You know Slade?" Chako asked with a frown of disapproval.

Slocum nodded—gently lying her down. "They must have been desperate for someone to drive to have sent him."

"The stage driver was killed . . . ," she managed.

Slocum blinked at the groggy-looking girl as she tried to get up. He pushed her back down. "Take it easy." He took the canteen that Chako had recovered for him and held it to her lips. "Sip it."

Chako squatted close by, obviously fascinated by her looks. "She's pretty."

"Yes," Slocum agreed and wet the kerchief from around his neck then wiped her face. "This should help cool you. When did you have any water last?"

"I had some barrel cactus yesterday."

He stopped and cocked a questioning eyebrow at her. "How did you know about them?"

"Mr. Slade had told me."

Back to cleaning her face, he shook his head. "Me and this Apache here wondered why they ever sent you this direction with Jed Slade anyway. I expect you didn't know it, but he was about the most worthless individual in his country. If he's dead, he damn sure won't be missed."

Chako nodded and grinned.

She sat up and shook her long, tangled golden hair, sweeping it back from her face. Then from her pocket she brought out a ribbon to tie it back. "I must agree he was a most despicable man. Thank you, I do feel better. I have no idea. Except the little stage man in Lordsburg had a lot of trouble finding a driver to take me, my luggage and the mail sacks on to Bowie."

"I see. I've got some crackers and dry cheese," he said, going to his saddlebags. "Some food might help you recover some strength."

"Thank you, Mr. Slocum. I have only fainted twice in my entire life. Once when I discovered Mr. Slade was dead, and here just a moment ago."

She rose on her knees. A demure-looking young woman despite all her problems, and she accepted his food offering. "Thank you, Mr. Slocum."

"Slocum. No mister, ma'am."

"Mary is fine. What do you and Chako do out here?"

"Right now we are scouting for some bucks run off from San Carlos and are headed for Mexico."

"Did they attack the stage station?" she asked, wiping any crumbs from her mouth.

"No, that was Mexican bandits."

"Wild Indians and bandits out here too?"

Slocum squatted down and nodded gravely. "To be truthful, you haven't chosen the best neighborhood to live in."

"Guess I am learning. These crackers taste very good."

"I suspect anything would taste very good to you right now."

They both laughed, and even Chako smiled, still watching her close.

"You get through eating, you can ride Chako's horse and

we'll ride Roan double. We can have you in Bowie"—he checked the sun time—"oh, a little after suppertime."

"That will be very generous. I guess all my books and clothing are lost?"

"We'll find them, if some two-legged pack rat doesn't find them first, and we'll bring them to you."

"I hope you find them. I'll be most grateful."

Chako nodded in agreement. "We find them." Seeing they were ready to leave, he rushed off for his pony.

The sun was a red fire on the horizon when they rode up the dusty street into Bowie. Not much to the small settlement. Three bars, two stores, a saddle maker and gunsmith, one blacksmith and a few adobe jacals all waiting for the much promised Southern Pacific tracks to arrive. Slocum read the disappointment on her face when he looked aside at her.

"Sure ain't much," he said and motioned to the store ahead. "That's John Jenks's store, he's the man sent for you."

"Yes. Good," she said, but he wondered what she really thought looking so skeptically at her new surroundings.

"They should have an eastbound stage through here in the morning," Slocum offered after Chako jumped off from behind him and he dismounted to take the reins of her horse.

"You think I should do that?"

"No, that's your business. But since it obviously was misrepresented, it might be one thing to consider."

"This is hardly a town—or anything." She dropped her gaze to the ground. "I have no clothing. My books, my personal things . . ."

"We'll go in the morning and search for them."

"Oh, I am so in your debt now—but you and Chako have work to do."

"Don't worry about us. We'll find them. You go inside, meet Jenks and his wife. They're nice people and will treat you well."

"But I look so—"

"Ain't no way you can help that." He hitched the horses and gave a head toss toward the open door.

She carried her skirts past him, shaking her head. "This could not have turned out worse."

"Oh, yes, it could have. And I don't need to draw no pictures for you."

On the wooden boardwalk she paused, chewed on her lower lip in consideration of what he'd said and then nodded in agreement before going inside.

"May I help you?" the whiskered man behind the counter asked, looking puzzled at her and Slocum.

"I'm Mary Harbor."

"Oh. Miss Harbor, W-what happened to you?" He looked appalled.

"Oh, it's a long story—too long to tell now. If you have a place I might clean up?"

"Certainly—Maggie, come. Maggie, come quick. Our new schoolmarm is here and she needs you."

"My dear, you look exhausted," the shorter woman with gray hair said, when she came in the room and hugged her. Then with a nod to Slocum, she took her protectively in the back.

"What happened to her?" Jenks asked in a stage whisper.

Slocum shook his head and then began the story of her and Jed Slade and finished with "She spent two days by herself in the desert before we found her."

"Wonder she's alive." Jenks shook his head in dismay. "It's so hard to get a teacher out here, I sure hope she stays."

"No telling. Chako and I've got to swing by Fort Bowie and see the colonel tonight. We'll go look for her things tomorrow."

"You figure that fall really killed Slade?" Jenks asked.

"I'm not sure, but she felt he was dead when she left him."

"I won't miss him."

"There won't be no one I know'll cry if he ever does have a funeral. Tell her we'll be back."

"Oh, yes. And, Slocum, thanks."

Two hours later, Slocum sat in Colonel Andrew Woolard's living room, sipping good Kentucky whiskey. Through the lace curtains he could see the empty Fort Bowie parade ground in the starlight. He'd told the fort's commander about Mary Harbor and finding her.

"My heavens, man, chances of that are one in a thousand, aren't they?"

"Close to that; she's a lovely young lady. And shocked at her first sight that Bowie was not a prosperous farming community like you'd find in the Midwest, I guess."

"Oh, that's no exaggeration, I am certain. And no sign of the runaways either?"

Slocum shook his head then tasted the whiskey—very smooth. "Chako thinks they may be laying low between here and the San Carlos Agency because they expect a band to come up from the Madres to get them and then make a raid up here."

"New theory, huh?"

"That boy knows lots about his people. Secondly, if they'd been through here on the east side of the Chiricahuas, he'd've already cut their trail."

Woolard nodded in agreement. "He can track a titmouse over a rock, I believe you said once of him." The colonel laughed and raised his glass. "Here's to Indian wars. The only damned thing we have."

"To Indian wars," Slocum said and they clinked glasses. "I'd like your permission to look for the runaway team and rig for her things and the mailbags. We should find them in a couple of days."

"Go find them. Besides, an intelligent young lady in the region might brighten the sour faces on my younger officers."

"Might." The recalled image of the beautiful young woman warmed him more than the whiskey. He finished his drink, thanked Woolard and went outside. After a cordial parting between them, he mounted Roan and turned him west. Chako would be waiting for him at the big spring in the draw.

He drew up near the large tanks in the shadowy night and his scout stepped out cradling a rifle in his arms.

"What did you learn?" Slocum asked, dropping heavy from the saddle.

"Two Dollar and Yellow Boy visited a squaw here today."

Several of the scouts and their families lived in a small village a quarter mile above the spring. Slocum had sent Chako up there earlier to find out what he could.

He let the roan drink his fill. "Why didn't some of them arrest those two?"

Chako shook his head. "They didn't know they had come by till they were gone."

"How did they know then?"

"They got Chewy's woman drunk and fucked her."

"Can we find their tracks in the morning?"

Chako nodded. "Big Jim and Chewy want to go too."

Slocum was torn between this and going after the runaway team and her things—but getting the two renegades was more important. Besides, Big Jim and Chewy if sent by themselves would only bring the two heads back in a gunnysack—he wanted information from them about those bronco Apaches down in the Sierra Madres. Caliche was the one leading the young bucks down there, and if he had plans to raid across the border, Woolard needed to know. They'd better see if they could track down the two bucks; then they'd look for the team.

"Chewy's mad over the deal?"

Chako nodded and grinned in the starlight. "They stole all her jewelry and left her bare-assed naked passed out in the wash."

Slocum chuckled. "I see why he's pissed. After sunup we'll figure out where they went. Better catch some sleep."

"We taking them two?"

"That's fine. We need to find those broncos."

Chako nodded. "They be here at dawn."

"Fine," Slocum said, getting a slab of jerky out of his saddlebags and holding it in his teeth while he undid his bedroll. He slung the roll down and then jerked loose the latigos. Cinches undone, he pulled off the saddle and piled it on the horn.

"I'll hobble him," Chako said.

"You eat?"

Chako bobbed his head. "Blue Quail had some sheep stew."

Slocum nodded and gnawed on the peppery, salvia-softened jerky. The woman's stew probably tasted lots better than his supper. Oh, well, maybe they'd find a better meal in the morning. Damn, he couldn't shake Mary's image from his mind.

2

Slocum nested a tin cup of hot coffee in his hands against the night's chill. The taller scout, Big Jim, came slipping in followed by Chewy. They squatted down and held their dark hands out to the fire.

"Get some coffee," Slocum said.

Big Jim nodded and looked around.

Slocum knew what he wanted. "No sugar. Chako ate it all."

The pair grunted and produced tin cans for cups that they filled from the pot hanging over the fire. Slocum wanted to laugh—Apaches drank sugar with coffee added if they got the chance.

"Your wife all right, Chewy?"

"Huh," the shorter buck grunted as he squatted across the small, smoky fire in his knee-high Apache boots. "Plenty hungover. I beat her ass good when I get back."

"The army won't like that."

Chewy scowled at him. "The army won't make her stop fucking them young bucks come around with whiskey, will they?"

"No."

"I will." Chewy raised the tin can with both hands to sip the coffee.

Big Jim nodded and drank some of his.

Chako brought their horses back from watering them, and

13

they went to scraping dirt onto the fire with the sides of their footwear. Finished, Slocum tied his cup on the pommel of his saddle, then checked the girths before stepping aboard. He let Big Jim take the lead, and he held back with a nod of approval at Chako for him to go ahead too.

For his money, the Apaches could be too damn talkative at times. Otherwise Slocum had to read their minds. This morning he knew they were going where the renegades had left Chewy's vanquished wife, to take up the tracks.

In thirty minutes, Slocum learned that the missing pair had some horses—unshod and one had a split hoof or two and wouldn't travel well in the rocky Chiricahua Mountains that reared up to their left. Big Jim mentioned that the broncos would stay close to the mountains until they could steal better ones. The other two Indians agreed, and with Slocum on their heels, they began to lope through the juniper-studded country spiked with century and yucca stalks.

Buster Rankin and his boys lived on Turkey Creek and ran a steam sawmill. Mid-morning they reached Buster's place. The whine of the big blade digging in the pine log filled the air, and the big man in a red plaid shirt shut it down and came out of the open shed to greet them. None of his sons were about.

"Buster, have you seen two bucks ride by?" Slocum asked. resting his forearm on the saddle horn.

"Was they riding two damn dink ponies?" the big man asked, brushing the wet sawdust off the front of his shirt.

"Have split hooves?" Big Jim asked.

"Split hooves, wind-broke sonsabitches. They took two of mine and left them in trade, I guess. They won't make soap."

"What time did they do that?" Slocum asked.

"Before I got up this morning. The damn dogs was raising hell and I got the gun and went to see what had them upset. But them bucks were riding off on them already. Never got a shot at them. Boy, that pissed me off."

Slocum laughed. "You and Chewy are in the same company. They fucked his wife and took all her jewelry last night."

The Apaches laughed softly, rocking in their saddles and nodding at each other.

Buster shook his head and laughed with them. "That would have pissed me off worse than stealing my horses. They're gone to Mexico now."

With a grim set to his mouth, Slocum looked south toward the Muleshoe Mountains. Fresh horses and that much of a lead, they'd never catch them. "You're right. Boys, let's go back."

"Climb down. I'll feed you all. Least I can do for the damn army."

"Mighty nice of you, Buster," Slocum said and dropped out of the saddle. His sea legs held, and after he adjusted the Colt in the holster, he undid the cinches.

"Maudie Ann, we got boarders," Buster shouted at the low-walled cabin.

A large, buxom woman in an apron came to the door and nodded. "Just what I've been waiting for." That and a spit off the edge of the porch and she went back inside.

"What've you been up to?" Buster asked Slocum as they headed for the horse tank to wash up.

"Looking for them two and they slipped past us."

"Hell, they do that all the time. Got 'em a damn railroad up and down through here."

"We only know about the ones they report as runaways."

Buster nodded before he cupped up some water from the tank and doused his face. Then he pulled loose the kerchief from around his neck to dry it and his hands.

Slocum did the same thing,

Kerchief tied back, Buster shook his head. "Hell, they sneak by here all the time."

"We may have to set up a few soldiers from Fort Huchuchua over here to be on the lookout."

"I'll take 'em. Them buffalo soldiers can sure play some mighty fine music."

"I'll tell Colonel Woolard."

"Good. Maybe I'll be able to keep some saddle stock then. Have a seat on the porch, boys," Buster said to the scouts. "She'll bring us out plates when she gets it done."

The rich meal of beef, tortillas and frijoles over, Slocum

wiped his mouth after setting aside the plate. "Thanks. Tell her it was good food. I told Chako we'd get some good grub today."

"You boys come by anytime,"

"Thanks, Buster. We need to head back and find a buckboard."

"Buckboard?"

"Yeah, one. They used it for the Lordsburg stage the other day. Horses ran off and left the passenger afoot."

"Good luck."

"We'll probably need it." Slocum looked off at the lofty Chiricahuas. It would be dark getting back to Bowie. They'd need to start out in the morning in their search.

"What did I hear about Mexican bandits?" Buster asked.

"They burned a stage stop and killed the operator. Made it look like Apaches did it, but some old prospector hid out in the tall grass and saw them. They were Mexicans."

"Well, damn, ain't that a hoot. Messicans acting like Apaches. What next?"

"His name is Fernando Diaz," Chako added.

Buster shook his head. "Don't know him. But he's giving old man Clanton some competition, huh?"

"Not yet," Slocum said and frowned. "Diaz don't have the army beef contract so far."

"You got the same feelings I have about that old pirate Clanton."

"The quartermaster says Clanton's man is the best source of beef he can find."

"I would be too if all I had to do was rustle it," Buster said.

The sawmiller joined Slocum in his walk to the horses. "Send word if you can if they have a big breakout of San Carlos. I'm right on the tracks."

"We will. Thanks again." Slocum shook the man's hand.

When he swung in the saddle, he noticed Chewy looking hard to the south. "You considering something?"

"I'll get them." The short, grim-faced scout reined his pony around.

Slocum nodded. "Don't blame you."

Big Jim and Chako snickered. Slocum didn't dare; he booted Roan out into a lope and kept the grin to himself.

Late afternoon he swung by Fort Bowie and spoke to Colonel Woolard. The officer laughed over the Chewy/wife deal and shook his head when Slocum told him about the horse theft.

"I hate they got back to the broncos, but they didn't kill anyone on the way, so aside from Chewy's wife's affair, I consider us lucky. I'll have them send Buster a company of black troopers to keep an eye on things. Tombstone needs his lumber for the mines and all the building going on."

Slocum agreed. "Chako and I are going buckboard hunting in the morning."

"Fine. Get that young lady fixed up."

"Yes, sir."

"I sent word for her to attend our monthly dance in two weeks."

"She'll be the hit of the party."

"Good, we need a hit out here. Be careful. No word on them coming up for a raid is there?"

"I haven't heard anything."

"I don't need any surprises. General Crook will be back down here in two weeks."

Slocum nodded he understood—Nantan Lupan didn't like surprises. The Apache called Crook the Gray Wolf. But he had lots of influence on them and really was the only one in command who understood how to fight them—Apache scouts. But Slocum knew as he took leave of the colonel that Crook had to constantly fight with upper command over his usage of them.

In the starlight he joined Chako in the spring draw. His horse hobbled and bedroll unrolled, he sat on his butt on top of it and pulled off his boots, to the relief of his feet.

"Hear anything?" he asked, rubbing his bare feet to increase the circulation and soothe them.

"No."

"We better get some sleep. We need to find that buckboard tomorrow."

"We find it."

"Yes." That said, Slocum slipped under the top blanket. By dawn it would be chilly in the arroyo. He soon was asleep.

In the night, he awoke and blinked to the sound of a woman

close by giggling. Easy-like, with his hand on the butt of his gun, he rolled over and could see the outline of Chako pumping away between her raised knees. She issued more giggles of pleasure as the scout pounded her harder, and then she wrapped her legs around him, raising her butt off the ground. Both were rasping for their breath as Chako's back straightened and he drove his dick home. Slocum turned back over—*just so Chewy didn't find out.*

3

In the midday sun, Slocum and Chako squatted in the shade of a mesquite. They were looking at a makeshift camp. Two wagons with bows covered in tattered yellow canvas covers were parked with several oxen grazing nearby. A ramada had been made with a tarp on poles. Slocum could see some women moving about a cooking fire. The buckboard they'd traced for hours was sitting unhitched, but the horses were not in sight.

"See any men?" Slocum asked his scout beside him.

Chako shook his head.

"I sure don't want to ride into a hornet's nest. Some of these hardscrabblers are really outlaws moving west. They may feel that buckboard is theirs."

"I go around and come in from back?" His scout waited for approval.

"Good idea. Keep your rifle ready. We don't need any shooting unless they blow up."

"Where they come from?"

"Lord only knows. But they look like trouble."

Chako took off in a low run. Slocum went back for his horse. He booted Roan off the ridge and let them see him coming downhill. A child or two in the camp shouted—"Some-un's coming."

Sunbonnets turned to look in his direction, and the older ones gathered in a cluster. Children ran to hide in dresses like

19

chicks hid under a hen. Still no men appeared, and Slocum wondered about that fact.

"Morning," Slocum said.

A hawkeyed woman with a sharp chin, clenching a corncob pipe in her teeth, stepped away for the younger women. "State your business."

"I'm looking for a team, buckboard, some mail and luggage."

She took the pipe out and her gray blue eyes glared at him. "They ain't here."

"You mind if I look at that buckboard?"

"I damn sure do."

"I represent the U.S. Army."

"Don't mean shit to me." She used the stem of her pipe to point west. "You can ride right back where you came from."

"Can't," he said, setting the saddle and trying to keep his guard up enough in case any opposition broke out of the wagons. Two of the three younger women were more attractive and better dressed than the fortyish "boss." But they didn't look one bit more hospitable than her.

"Where are your menfolk?"

"None of you damn business."

"Ma'am, I'm going to look at that buckboard."

"Get out of here, 'fore I go get my shotgun—" At the sounds of Chako levering a cartridge in his Winchester behind her, she started and turned.

"Everyone stay put. Chako won't shoot you unless you try something."

Slocum waited a few seconds, until he was satisfied they would hold; then he pushed Roan over to the buckboard and dismounted. The rig belonged to the stage line. Their brand was on the back of the spring seat. But the mail and the luggage were nowhere in sight. He turned back and dismounted.

"Opening U.S. mail is a federal offense. Where is it?"

"You're so damn smart, find it."

"What's your name?"

"Claudia, Claudia Thorpe."

On a small notepad, he wrote it down in pencil. Then he

looked at the taller, rawboned woman beside her. "What's your name?"

"Sadie Slade."

He nodded after writing it down and looked at the prettier girl beside her. "Your name?"

"Wanda."

"Thorpe?"

"Yes."

"My name's Candy," the fourth one said, and took off her sunbonnet and shook out her black curls. "We don't know nothing about no mail, but if'n you were interested, you and I could get up in that wagon and talk about it." She rolled her dark eyelashes at him.

"Another time, another place, maybe," Slocum said as he strode past the tart.

He looked in the first wagon and saw an opened trunk with clothes sticking out of it. Obviously it had been rummaged through. He climbed inside and found that there were schoolbooks in the turned-up clothing. Those two—Candy and Wanda—had on new dresses, or at least nicer than the other two's soiled, wash-worn ones.

"This trunk belongs to Mary Harbor," he said and closed it up. He hefted it to the edge of the wagon and then transferred it to the ground.

"You two get those dresses off." He pointed at the pair. "Those dresses are hers too."

"No, they ain't," Mother Thorpe shouted.

"Either they can shed them or I'm taking you all in for theft."

"My men get back here—" Mother said, through her clenched teeth.

"Now where are the mailbags?" The two were unbuttoning the dresses. He was getting shots of white flesh as they deliberately stripped off the clothing before him.

"We ain't got none."

"I'm getting damn tired of your mouth."

"Aw, hell, tell him," the rawboned Sadie said.

"Shut your mouth, girl."

"No!" Slocum jerked Claudia around by the arm. "Tell me."

"In the other wagon . . ."

Slocum gave a head toss to Chako, who sprang to his feet and went to the other wagon's tailgate. He turned back and nodded.

"Here," Candy said, handing him the dress. "I never liked it anyway." Her bare teardrop breasts exposed, she shoved her pink nipples forward.

He took the dress and shook his head at the amused Chako, who tossed off two mailbags. On the ground, he picked up his rifle and nodded as if to say, *What're you doing next?*

"Better go find you some clothes," Slocum said to her.

"You don't like my titties?" She cupped her small pointed breasts and lifted them for him to see.

"I'm worried you're going to get a bad sunburn on 'em," he said and chuckled. Holy cow, two good-looking, half-naked women and he was playing marshal.

"Aw, you sure you and I can't go romp in the featherbed up there?" Candy asked with a head toss to the wagon.

"Not today. Where are the men and those horses?"

"They get back here, they'll stomp your ass in the ground," Mother Thorpe said. "You two little whores go get some damn clothes on."

"When're they coming back?" Slocum asked.

"How should I know?"

" 'Cause walking to Fort Bowie is a long way and you all will be walking there in ten minutes if your memory don't recover."

"They're due back anytime and they'll settle this. Making my girls strip naked and holding us hostage—you ain't met my man. You will."

"His name is?"

"Joshua Thorpe."

He turned to Sadie Slade. "And yours?"

"Jed."

Slocum stopped. "Thought he died."

Sadie wrinkled her red nose at him. "That bitch only thought she'd killed him."

"Well. It'll be interesting. Since he stole the buckboard and mail they hired him to haul to Bowie."

"You'll see when they get here," Mother shouted.

"I want all of you to go sit in the shade on the ground. Kids and all. One word of warning to them and I'll drop them dead in their tracks. You all understand?"

Even the two girls finished dressing, nodded and took their places under the wind-ruffled canvas top. Some of the small kids were crying and being hugged. Things settled, he took Chako aside, telling him to go scout for the men.

Then Slocum found a seat on a wooden crate behind them—with the rifle across his knees. The wait had begun. Candy sat facing him with her back against Wanda's. Soon she had her knees raised, with the tattered brown dress pulled up to expose her white legs, and she spread them apart every once in a while when he glanced at her, so he could see between the snowy bare legs—the patch of black pubic hair and the lips of her pink cunt when she parted them wide enough.

"How long you going to wait fur 'em?" Mother Thorpe asked.

"Till they get back."

"Hell, that might be next week."

"Where did they go with the horses?"

"I said, I didn't know—"

"Hush, they're coming back," he said at the sounds of some horses approaching.

Two riders came in on sweaty horses and they dropped off them in a cloud of dust.

"What the hell are you all sitting around for?" the big bearded man shouted at the women, coming around the front of his horse.

"'Cause I told them to. Both of you grab some sky or die!"

"What the shit—" Slade, with his head bandaged, spun around, his hand poised for his gun butt. At the last moment, he decided to raise his hands high along with Thorpe.

"Rustling horses, U.S. mail theft, attempted rape and stealing a stage."

"You the damn law?" Thorpe asked from behind the black woolly beard, looking like a mad bear woke up from hibernation.

Slade shook his head in grim assessment. "I guess that damn bitch didn't die after all."

"No thanks to you." Slocum shook his face in regret that Slade hadn't been killed.

Chako rode in and bounded off his pony.

"Tie 'em up. They're going to Bowie."

"I can do that." The scout jerked out their six-guns and knives to discard them on the ground in Slocum's direction. In a short while, the two were thrust up, hands behind them, and sitting on the ground. With Chako guarding them and the women, Slocum harnessed the team. Mary's things and the mail finally loaded, he put the grumbling pair in the back and roped them down to the bed.

"What now?" Chako asked when they finished.

"Go unload her shotgun that's in one of these wagons, so she don't shoot us in the back," he said in a stage whisper.

"She need it?"

"Might. Just unload it and hide the shells."

He had their handguns and knives in a sack and put them on the buckboard.

"Gawdamn you, Slocum!" Slade shouted and kicked at him.

"Listen, I can bust you over the head and you won't be so damn belligerent on this ride. Think about it before you kick or cuss at me again."

Thorpe's eyes narrowed to slits as he fought at his binds. "I'll get you."

"When you get out of prison, you'll be too old to catch a tortoise."

"You'll see. You'll see."

Slocum tied the roan to the tailgate. "I'll be watching real close twenty years from now."

He looked at the hard-eyed women getting up and brushing the dirt off their butts. He took a seat next to Chako, then the reins in his hands and nodded. "Have a nice day, ladies."

"Fuck you!" Mother Thorpe shouted at him

The mail sacks and her things were left off at the Bowie post office. Slocum saw no sign of Mary, and anxious to deliver his grumbling prisoners, he told the stage man that a soldier would bring back the buckboard and horses.

"Hell, Slocum, we're just damn glad you got the mail, her things and them two bastards in custody. I'm putting you in for the fifty dollars reward the stage line pays."

On the seat, he considered the possible publicity and shook his head. "Pay Chako here that money."

"What's his last name?"

"Ah . . ." He looked over at the scout and winked. "Chako Smith."

"I'll get it for him."

"Good." Slocum wheeled the horses around and headed in the bleeding light for Bowie. Be long past dark before they got there. When he slapped the horses to set them in a trot, he regretted not getting to look at Mary again. Damn business anyway.

At Bowie, the officer of the day, Captain Casey, had two soldiers take the grumpy pair to the brig and then he filled out the report for Slocum to sign. A seasoned veteran, Casey was a proficient man to do all the necessary papers, and after dipping the straight pen and signing it, Slocum thanked him.

"Hell, you did all the work. The colonel will be pleased. I'll tell him in the morning."

"Chako and I may go to the border tomorrow and see what we can find out."

"I'll tell him that too."

Slocum nodded and shook his hand. It had been a long day. He stepped outside, past the sentries into the starlight. Chako handed him the reins to his horse and he bounded into the saddle.

Slocum saluted Casey on the porch and rode off into the night. Why did he think that he had not seen the last of those two outlaws? Something about their threats and the fact that Slade had survived—even with them in the Fort Bowie brig, Slocum felt niggled over something. He finally shrugged it off when they reached the springs and he hobbled his horse, strung out his bedroll and went to sleep without supper.

He awoke with a sergeant squatted beside him. Slocum sat up and tried to clear his eyes. "Colonel wants you to find out all you can about Diaz while you're down there."

"Fine, we will."

"Sorry I had to wake you. He was worried you'd be leaving early."

Slocum scrubbed his beard stubble in his callused palms and nodded. "Good idea. I get anything on Diaz, I'll send him word."

"I'll tell him. He said for you to keep your head down, and the U.S. marshal would be coming for them two."

"Taking them to Tucson?"

"Yes. Why?"

Slocum only nodded and then dismissed it with a headshake. That was what was wrong. Why he'd been so upset about them. That tin-can jail in Tucson wouldn't hold those two for no time. He sighed and then threw back the covers to pull on his boots. "Thanks for the good news."

"Good news?"

"If they're still in jail in a week over there, I'll buy you a beer."

The noncom grinned. "I'll tell the colonel."

Slocum frowned aside at him. "He won't be in charge."

"Might up my chances of getting a free one." The noncom laughed and left him.

Slocum's breakfast consisted of pepper-hot, tough jerky as he and Chako rode south. They made lunch with Maudie Ann Rankin, which improved his disposition. That evening they reached Birch Turner's ranch before dark. A tall, hulking Texan that even old man Clanton left alone, Turner operated the T Cross ranch on the south slopes of the Muleshoes with his wife Billie and a half dozen Mexican vaqueros. A tough enough individual that the Apaches avoided him, Birch smiled and nodded when he came out on the porch of the stone house to greet Slocum and Chako.

"How have you been?" Slocum asked, shaking his huge hand before he undid his latigos. The slow-drawling, big man was always a good one to visit—he never seemed to do anything too fast, but Slocum had not seen him in action. Word was he'd single-handedly killed five Mexican rustlers in a box canyon one day when he caught them changing brands on some of his stock.

"Aw, all right. How you and that buck getting on?"

"Fine. We arrested Jed Slade and a guy named Thorpe yesterday."

"That damn worthless Slade needs hung. I caught him twice taking whiskey to the broncos. I busted it up, and the last time I told him he come through here again with that crap I'd string him up."

"Must be why he's been working on the east side."

"Could be. Jerk them saddles off. Billie's got some frijoles hot."

"Okay. You seen any broncos headed south?"

"Jua-loo saw two of 'em a day or so ago hotfooting it for the Madres."

"They were riding Buster Rankin's horses."

Birch laughed. "Better his ponies than mine. They stole a dozen of old man Clanton's best horses the week before. Heard him cussing plumb up here." Then he chuckled deep in his throat. "Beats the hell out of me how a handful of the bucks can outdo the Mexican Army, ruralists, U.S. Army and all the rest."

"They've been outdoing the Mexicans for two hundred years." Slocum put Roan in the corral, and Chako did the same with his pony.

"Them horses will be fine in that lot. There's hay and a tank in there." Birch closed the gate and hooked it. "Yah, but them Messikins never were this serious before now."

"You ever crossed swords with some bandit named Diaz?" Slocum asked as they headed for the house.

"*General?*"

"Maybe—he raided a stage stop over near the New Mexico line. Made it look like Apaches, but there was a witness said it was Mexican bandits."

Birch nodded in the light escaping from the open door. "I figured all along this talk about Apache raiding might have been more than they could do."

"Wonder where Diaz is at."

"I heard he had a hacienda in the Conchos."

Slocum frowned. There wasn't much of nothing in those hills. "That ain't a very prosperous place."

"Easy to defend a stronghold there. Billie," Birch called out, "that rascal Slocum and his scout Chako are here for supper."

"Shucks, Birch, he ain't no rascal," The gray-haired, willowy woman rushed over and hugged him tight. "My, my, where have you been?"

"Army's working me too hard."

"Well," she said, leaning back and looking him over from head to toe. "They ain't overfed you none." With a wary headshake, she led him and Chako to the table. "Food's hot. Have a seat and I'll be right back."

"What ja going to do about Diaz?" Birch asked in his deep drawl.

"Scout him, I guess, is all. Maybe he'll slip back up here and I can cut him off."

The rancher shook his head. "Mexican bandits and bronco Apaches—throw in old man Clanton and hell might be a nice address to have."

"Clanton giving you any trouble?"

"Naw, but having that many cattle rustlers in your backyard is like living next door to a den of wolves."

"Guess he's finding enough cattle in Mexico to steal to fill all his government contracts."

"He's bought some up here to finish out some contracts, I figure. Course they average out cheap with the free ones." Birch chuckled deep in his throat. "Aw, you boys eat now," he said as she brought them heaping plates of beef, beans, and flour tortillas.

The next morning, after a big breakfast and thanking their hosts, Slocum and Chako rode on. They dropped off into the Santa Cruz River Valley and headed into Mexico. Near sundown they reached a small cluster of jacals called Saint Francis. No church there, but Slocum always thought the name came from the wishes of the earliest settler that maybe if they named it that, the early Spanish church builder Father Kino would put one there. Kino never did.

In the dim twilight, a barefoot woman stood in the doorway of a run-down adobe hut, smoking a corn-husk cigarette. She nodded when they rode up.

"Could a starving man buy supper here?" Slocum asked in Spanish, sitting his horse.

She threw the cigarette down and ground it under her sole. "If he had any money."

"Oh, we have *mucho dinero*."

"You look like beggars to me." Then she laughed and ran over to hug him when he dismounted. Her large breasts jammed into his stomach, she threw her head back to clear the wavy hair from her face and looked up. "Where have you been so long?"

"Trying to get back here." He slid his hands along her cheeks until he clutched her face and then held it as he kissed her. She parted her lips and teeth so his tongue sought hers, and her arms tightened around him. She pressed her hips to him so her lower stomach was hard against his upper right leg. Then she separated her legs so she could rub her mound on him. Fire began to come from her nostrils, and when their mouths parted, she sucked for air.

"Mother of God, Slocum—you want food?"

He looked down in the dark pools under long lashes and slow-like he nodded. "Me and my pard ain't ate since before sunup."

She buried her face in his shirt and snuggled against him. "All right, I will find you some."

"Wonderful. Tell me what you've been doing." His arm over her shoulder, they started inside. Chako pointed to the horses, indicating he'd put them up, and Slocum agreed with a nod.

"Doing in this place? Existing is a better word. Nothing."

"Aw, bet you've been partying every night."

"Partying? Ha, they never have a fandango here anymore."

"This used to be a live place." Slocum took a seat on the palette she showed him.

"The young men are all gone or killed," she said, bent over

the fireplace, feeding it small sticks to start her cooking fire again. "Only the old men with weak dicks are left here. No, this place is dead for me."

Straightening, she shifted the low-necked blouse so the deep V showed, as well as the firm tops of her cleavage. Theresa Montez was in her late twenties, widowed by a knife fight in a border bar that took her young husband Valentine. She'd worked in the whorehouses up there in the territory for a few years; then an old man named Arnold offered her a job cooking at his mine. Slocum met her there—Arnold was killed by bandits and Slocum brought them to justice. Then he made sure she was awarded enough of Arnold's estate to live on and she moved to St. Francis.

"What are you doing down here anyway?" she asked, twisting around to look at him.

"Looking for broncos and," he lowered his voice, "checking on a bandit named Diaz."

She frowned at him for a second then nodded. "The broncos I hope stay in the mother mountains, and Diaz is a big bag of wind with the dick of small pig."

He chuckled. "You know him then?"

She wrinkled her nose and knelt down on her knees to make tortillas. "I knew him five years ago in Nogales. He swaggered around and told all the girls that worked there in the Loso Luna, 'I have a dick like donkey.'" She shook her head in disgust and put the first tortilla on the griddle. "Big as my small finger." She held it up in the candlelight to demonstrate the size and then laughed. "Oh, the *grande* Colonel Diaz is a mean, dumb ass donkey."

"He made a raid over the border and tried to make it look like Apaches did it."

She shook her head, patting out the tortilla between her palms. "He has a place they say in the Conchos."

"A grand hacienda?"

She wrinkled her nose. "Probably some straw wickiups left by the Apaches."

He nodded that he'd heard her. Then he looked up when

Chako came to the doorway. He motioned for the Apache to join them.

"Chako—Theresa."

They both nodded to each other and the scout sat down beside him.

"She doesn't think Diaz has a great place in the Conchos."

"I think it is at an old rancheria. I was there once a long time ago."

"Yes," she said and her face brightened. "The Arterio ranch. There was a spring there."

"Big spring," Chako said and grinned. "I can remember swimming in the tank."

"Cold too."

"Ah, very cold."

"Good," Slocum said. "We'll go see what we can find at this cold spring."

Her brown finger waved at him in warning. "You must be careful going there. He may have a small dick, but he would kill you fast as this." She drew her hand across her throat.

"Yes, we are always careful."

On her knees making more tortillas for them, she looked at the ceiling for God's help. "Not always."

After her meal, Chako slipped away in the night. No telling where he might put his bedroll. Slocum didn't worry about the boy; Chako slept with one eye open and at a good vantage point when they were away from the safer places.

"I must bathe before we go to bed," she said and blew out the flickering candles.

He watched her in the dim light, studying the curves of her small supple body as she washed over the surfaces, and each time dipped her cloth in a pan, then wrung it out. At last she wrapped herself in thin robe and held out her hand to him.

"We have business to finish," she said in a husky voice.

"Yes."

"I have a great bed outside. Come. I have dreamed of your return to me."

He followed her out into the night full of crickets and chirping sounds. Under the paloverde, the hammock looked inviting in the filtered starlight. She helped him undress, putting his gun and holster, then his clothes over a straight-back chair as he handed them to her. At last with him naked, she opened the shift and pressed her skin to his and hugged him. He felt her warm breath on the top of his breastbone and her small fingers fondling his genitals.

"Oh, Slocum, I would go where you say."

He hugged her to him. "But I wouldn't know where to tell you to meet me."

"I know. Those two deputies have been here twice looking for you. The Abbots."

Slocum frowned at her over the information. "They haven't hurt you?"

"No." She pressed her face to him. "They must never get tired of looking for you."

His hands massaging her rock-hard butt, he shook his head. "Never."

"Get in bed," she whispered and gave him a nudge. "We can talk about that later."

He let her get on first and then he joined her atop the springy swing. She acted anxious to begin. She made him get over her and between her knees. Scooted down under him, she drew hard on his hardening erection. Raising her butt up she inserted him in the moist gates.

Slocum felt his chest tighten and a great urgency rise in his hips as he eased his dick through the ring and began to pump her. In pleasure's arms, she threw her head back. The shadowy light showed her mouth open in ecstasy's relief. The soft moans from her throat spurred him onward.

His prick began to swell rock hard and her ring began to contract. Soon waves of contractions began to meet his thrusts into her pleasure palace. Her small hands clutched him as their world began to spin away into space beyond their surroundings under the stars. The place where the guttural sounds from their throats matched the efforts of two athletic bodies in their drive for some new plateau as one. Where nothing else existed, but his rock-hard sword plunging into her fiery body again and again. Until all was skin stretched tight, to the point of pain, and a tingling in the bottom of his scrotum, drawing all of his strength for its force, then exploding like a volcano out of the splintered head of his dick. And then they collapsed in a spent pile.

"Mother of God," she whispered and hugged him tight. "Oh, my lover, I want to hold you forever."

He chuckled and pushed his weight off of her. "Ah, Theresa. We always could make love."

"But sometimes I forget—" Then she began to pull on his slick, dying erection. "Do it once more, my lover. Then I will let you sleep."

He bent over and kissed her forehead. "Once more." Then he looked to the stars filtered by the paloverde foliage for help. But her growing actions were reactivating him. In minutes, he was back inside her, easing in and out and grinning down at her as she tossed her head in pleasure's arms.

"Yes, yes," she whispered.

4

Diaz's ranch was tucked into a valley of palms. The mountains consisted of black to purple rocks, giving it a dark cast, and little grew on them but some greasewood and cactus. Any horse feed had to be brought in, Slocum decided, lying on his belly looking through his scope.

"The last ones kept too many goats and sheep," Chako said as if he had asked him.

"This used to be a goat and sheep ranch?"

The buck nodded his head, bellied down beside him.

"How many men are here?" He handed him the telescope.

"Only a handful."

"Where are the rest?" He could see the thatched roofs of the few buildings clustered near some pens and the sun reflected off the water in the large rock tank.

"He may gather them from other villages when he is ready to go on a raid."

"That's an idea. How many horses are there?"

"Only a handful." With a shake of his head, Chako dismissed them.

"Then if we steal them and then find his main herd, we can put him afoot."

The Apache grinned at the prospect of some excitement. "We could have fun trying."

"After dark we'll take them."

34

"Yes." Chako rolled back on his belly and looked intently through the eyepiece. "Mexicans are not as good as Americans as sentries. What will we do with the horses?"

"What if we give them to old man Clanton as a present?"

"Huh?"

"That would make Diaz think Clanton stole them and he can be mad at him."

Chako went to chuckling. "That *general* would find he had *el tigre* by the tail if he tried to attack Clanton, no?"

"Exactly. Can we do it?"

"I think so."

"Let's ride back to Saint Francis and get some sleep."

Chako collapsed the scope and agreed.

Midday, they arrived at Theresa's. She inquired about what they'd found and busied herself cooking food.

Slocum explained the plan.

"I want to go along. I can hold the horses, bring them to you when you need them." Excitement danced in her eyes. "It gets very boring in this village."

Slocum looked at Chako—he nodded as if he didn't care.

"All right, but we need to nap this afternoon. It will be a long, long ride. You know where he keeps the rest of his horses?" he asked her.

"No. But there is a bosquet and tules north of there where there is some grass. I bet the other horses are up there."

"Chako, you know where she means?"

"Yes, that would be a good place."

"How far is Clanton's from there?"

"A long ways."

"One or two days?"

"Two."

"We can make that." Slocum grinned, satisfied. "It won't be easy, but we can do that."

"You are going to deliver them to Clanton?" she asked with a frown.

"I want Diaz to think he stole them."

"What for?"

"So the general takes Clanton on."

"Who will win?"

"Clanton—" Slocum shook his head and hugged her. "The old man has a hundred of the toughest, meanest gunmen in the West on his payroll. Diaz messes with him—he'll damn sure lose."

"And then Diaz won't raid over the border anymore?"

"Exactly."

She hugged him. "And the army sent you here to do this?"

"Only to look, but they'll unofficially like my plan."

"I am excited."

"It won't be easy and it will be dangerous."

"I understand. Come and eat. The frijoles are hot."

She packed them food and loaded some things on a mule he discovered when he awoke from his nap. Before the moon rose, they left her casa, with her riding a thin horse they promised to replace and leading the pack mule. It came at a trot so Slocum's concern about it keeping up soon evaporated.

They left her and their saddle stock in the canyon below the ranch. That would be the way out if they could get to the horses and drive them away from the headquarters.

"We get caught or anything goes wrong," Slocum said to her in the starlight, standing beside her stirrup, "you get the hell out of here and don't look back."

She glanced away.

He clapped her on the leg through the dress to get her attention. "Hear me?"

"Yes."

"Be damn sure you mind me."

"I will."

He nodded and took off on foot after his scout. Not any cover, so they kept to the wash, using it to keep their silhouettes out of sight. Chako led the way in the soft alluvial fill swept in by flash rains and spread over the bottom.

They soon reached the palms and eased out into the shadowy night among them. Night insects and men snoring were all that reached Slocum's ears. Obviously the camp was quiet. He saw no fires, and the place sat bathed in the pearl starlight, with the thatched roofs showing up like piles of snow.

"One guard at the corral," Chako whispered, giving a head toss in that direction.

Slocum nodded. He saw the man wandering around by the pen of horses as if to stay awake. Chako indicated he would go around—Slocum agreed.

In minutes, Chako was behind him and knocked him out with a swift blow to the head.

Looking both ways, Slocum broke from the palms to help him drag the unconscious sentry into the shadows. The youth bound and gagged at last, they listened and waited. Satisfied that nothing was astir, they took bridles from the fence and went into the corral. In minutes, they had two horses saddled and the gate open.

Hissing at the sleepy horses to make them move, they drove them out the opening and headed down the canyon at a trot. Slocum looked over his shoulder to check—nothing. They pushed the dozen horses ahead. The bosquet bunch was next if that was where they were grazing them.

"How far to this place where the rest of them might be?" Slocum asked his man.

"An hour."

He nodded and looked back. Diaz might be a blowhard, but he damn sure would be mad when he learned his horses were gone. And angry men made tough enemies. He wondered how many guarded the herd.

Theresa joined them. He swapped her saddle over and put her on his roan so she could keep up better than on her thin pony. A big smile creased her face when she reined the horse around.

"No trouble?"

He shook his head. "But we haven't stolen his main one yet either."

She wrinkled her nose at him. "I am not worried."

"That makes one of us," he said and booted his horse after the rest.

At the approaching dawn, he'd fretted about the big steal. Their capture went smoothly. The guards ran off at the first shots, and they had the herd moving north without a hitch. So easy Slocum looked over his shoulder all day for pursuit, but none came, the three of them driving the horses hard, with boiling telltale dust in the sky.

By the time the moon rose that night, Chako said they were getting close to Clanton's place. The horses were dropping their heads in the dust, exhausted. A few had even slowed and quit, but most were holding a trot in the bunch.

With the three of them waving their ropes to keep them moving, Slocum rode over to his man. "When we get within a quarter mile, we'll go to shooting and raising hell so they stream in there."

"Good idea," she said, pulling up with them. "Reckon he'll think God sent him these horses?"

Slocum shook his head. "He knows God ain't doing anything for him."

The time grew near. The horses were snorting a lot. He'd caught her horse out so they would not identify it. They switched mounts; he left the saddle from the ranch on the black, and Chako did the same when he caught his own pony out and they put both of in with the herd.

"EEHA!" Slocum screamed and went to shooting. The herd threw up its head and flew toward the dark outline of the old man's big house. Firing wild gunshots, he and Chako took the wings and she rode drag. The herd was going full-tilt when they reined up to let them go on. Lights came on, and shots flashed in the night.

Someone screamed, "Apaches! Apaches!" More shots and lots of cussing, but Slocum and company were jogging northwest as fast as their ponies would go and laughing. Soon all the noise and excitement was behind them—they reached Fort Bowie mid-morning. Slocum showed his papers and then had the sergeant in charge of the stables have his men on duty rub down and grain their horses plus her mule.

They walked to the closest café and Slocum bought them breakfast.

"I'll send the colonel a note on what we found." Between bites, he explained the future plan. "Maybe he has word on the broncos."

Chako looked at him over the steaming coffee mug he held in both hands. "What then?"

"Damned if I know. He'll have a new plan for us."

The scout shook his head at her. "They always work. These white men. No time to play."

"He better find some, huh?" She smiled big back at Chako.

"That's why I didn't send him a damn telegram yet," Slocum said.

"Oh," she said and ducked with a grin to cut her eggs with the fork.

"We'll meet back here at sunup at the stables," he said to Chako.

The scout agreed and disappeared when the meal was over. Slocum knew some better places to rest and relax than some bedbug-riddled hotel around the fort's perimeter. The outpost was high enough in elevation and the mountains that backed it to grow pines. She agreed, and with a blanket roll, canteen of water, bottle of whiskey and some of her food, they set out on foot. In a short while they found a glen and made camp.

They needed nothing to rock them to sleep, and he awoke after sundown when a coyote cut loose. Extracting himself from her arms, he slipped off and emptied his bladder. Back and seated on the ground under the millions of stars, he opened the saddlebags and extracted a cold burrito. Taking a bite, he chewed on it slow-like and considered what lay ahead. Stealing Diaz's horses he knew wouldn't make the bandit quit—and any day, Caliche and his bunch might try to bust back across the border to gather up more arms and ammo. Both of them needed to be settled, but he couldn't take on Diaz or Caliche without the army or a company of scouts, and they were still arguing over that between Washington and Mexico City.

She sat up and stretched in the starlight. "Well, *mi amigo*, you get rested?"

"Not yet." He took another bite from his burrito. "I could sleep for a week and not have enough rest."

"Well, I will be back." She gathered up her skirt and headed for the bushes. "I too could sleep a long time," she said over her shoulder

He nodded after her and blinked his gritty eyes. A week might not be enough.

After some lovemaking, they slipped back asleep, and only

awoke when the morning doves in the pine boughs heralded the coming dawn. Still bleary-eyed, he rolled up the blankets in the dim light and they headed back.

Chako squatted in the shadows when they reached the stables. He handed Slocum a paper. Slocum traded his bedroll and saddlebags for it. Turned to the coming dawn, he read the message:

> Wish I'd been there for the horse raid. No diplomatic news from Washington. If we can catch Diaz on this side of the border, it would be easier. Sergeant Malloy said you needed to know that Thorpe and Slade escaped the Tucson Jail. Nothing on the broncos either.
>
> Colonel Andrew Woolard

"What's he want us to do next?"

"Keep track of Diaz and Caliche."

"Same old stuff?"

He nodded to the scout. "We better take her home and then see what we can about the broncos."

"What about Diaz?" she asked, looking back and forth at them.

"It will take him that long to get new horses." Slocum chuckled and tied his saddlebags on his saddle.

"Maybe he can buy them back from old man Clanton." Chako winked at her.

"I doubt it," Slocum said and finished tightening his girth. "Let's have one more store-bought breakfast."

Both of them bobbed their heads.

By nightfall, they'd ridden up to her jacal in Saint Francis. Loaded with food and supplies he'd bought for her, her mule Domino honked loudly at his arrival. In the distance, more answered him. Slocum dropped out of the saddle and surveyed things. Nothing looked out of place. Satisfied—

It was the shrill whistle of a hawk that sent Slocum into action—Chako's signal that trouble was afoot. A figure stepped out into the dark doorway of her shack with a gun in his hand.

Slocum shoved the roan in front of her and ducked, drawing his own gun with his right hand. Shots broke the night. Slocum's bullets sent the one in the door stumbling backward.

To his left, Chako's rifle cut down another on the roof, and he pitched headfirst off the jacal to plop on the ground. Slocum turned an ear to someone running away.

"I'll get him," Chako said and was gone.

"Good." Slocum searched the night then knelt down beside her. "You all right?"

"Sure," she said quick-like and started to get up off her butt. "You shove hard."

"Sorry. I didn't want you in the way of his bullets."

"I know. I'm grateful. Who were they?"

"Banditos," a voice announced.

Slocum could see the outline of woman with her hands on her hips.

"That is my neighbor Madera," she said as Slocum pulled her to her feet.

"How many?" Slocum asked her.

"Three was all I see. They came this afternoon all mad about someone stealing their horses they said."

"How did they get here?"

"On some mules. They cussed them too."

"I wonder how in the hell they knew to come here." Slocum, gun ready, stepped to the doorway and heard the soft moans of the man lying on the floor. He struck a match and saw he had no gun in his hands, then went by and lit two candles. Then he squatted on the hard-packed floor beside the outlaw.

"How did you know to come here?"

"I'm . . . dying . . ." The man drew up in fetal position.

"I said who told you to come here?"

"Generale Diaz . . ."

"What did he know?"

". . . 's woman."

"What did he say?" he asked the two women standing over him and talking to each other in low voices. He reached over to shake more answers out of the outlaw—but knew it was no use. He was dead.

"There is spy in this village," Madera said in disgust and glanced at Theresa. "Who is the *puta* for those worthless bastards?"

Theresa shook her head and turned up her hands in surrender.

"I am going to get Don Jesus and make him find her," Madera said, pushing her graying hair back from her face. A woman of ample figure and hard eyes, she stomped off into the night to find the mayor.

"She'll have the place turned upside down to find her," Theresa said. "When she gets mad, nothing will stop her."

"Those bandits must have really insulted her," Slocum said.

"Worse than that—they took turns raping her this afternoon while waiting for us."

"Sumbitches. Didn't expect—" He looked up when Chako appeared in the doorway. "Get him?"

The scout nodded.

"Find their mules?"

"Three of them."

"Let's haul this one's carcass out of here." He indicated the dead one.

"Good," she said. "I'll make us some food."

Slocum and his scout were seated on the floor when Madera and the mayor returned. The snow-headed, small man nodded to Slocum when he came inside.

"Señor, we are sorry to cause your village any trouble," Slocum said. "We did not know there was a spy here."

"She will spy no more," he said with a cold edge in his voice. "Diaz has no spy here now."

"What can we do?"

"We will bury them so no one can find them. If you will take the mules so they cannot be traced here?"

"We will take them when we leave here."

"Maybe best if they are shot away from here. They might go home, and then he would know that the bandits died here."

"Maybe," Slocum agreed.

The two women talked at the side in whispers. The mayor refused Slocum's offer to join them to eat—he had things to see about—apologized and left. Madera went with him.

When they were gone, Theresa poured them coffee in mugs and then looked out the doorway into the night. "Madera said they garroted the *puta*. They take such things very serious here."

Slocum nodded that he heard her. The process they used was a noose placed around her neck; then with her back to her executioner, she was jerked to death when he bent over. A painful death by strangulation unless her neck was broken in the first jerk.

They ate supper in silence. Slocum broke the quiet. "Perhaps you should go with us. You may not be safe here. Hell only knows what Diaz knows about you."

She nodded and suppressed a grin. "Oh, I guess I could go along."

"Be damn good idea," Chako said, rubbing his belly. "We can use a real cook."

They laughed, and it broke up the seriousness of the situation.

5

"You want a mule to eat?" Slocum asked the man in sandals and threadbare, once white clothing, who stood straw hat in hand beside his broken-down ox cart. His dark-eyed children peeked around the *carreta* at this gringo on the roan horse with the mule on a lead rope.

The man wadded the ragged straw sombrero in his hands and nodded. "I would rather ride him."

"No, they would say you stole him. You savvy?" Slocum looked at the small pregnant woman who stood looking downcast at her swollen belly.

"I savvy," the man said quickly, lest Slocum changed his mind. "What must I do?"

"I will take him down there by the cottonwoods, shoot him and cut his throat. Do you have a good rope we can string him up with?"

"*Sí, señor.*"

"I'll haul him up so you can butcher him, too."

"Oh, *señor, gracias.*"

Sitting the roan, Slocum looked in disgust over the makeshift shade they'd set up to simply camp around the disabled cart. "Can you find a wheel or fix that broken one?"

"There is wheel in the next village, but it costs two pesos."

"Tell me the name of the man who has it."

"Lopez."

"I will pay for the wheel when I go through there. You can go get it tomorrow."

"I will be in your debt forever." His face lightened with excitement. "We go to a nice rancheria to work. Hear him, my darling? The fine señor will buy us a wheel for the *carreta*."

"And a mule to eat," Slocum said and took his ward down into the bottom under a stout-looking gnarled cottonwood. The man came running with a rope. Slocum dispatched the black mule with a bullet between the eyes and he dropped like a poled steer. Slocum stepped off on the ground and drew the skinning knife from behind his back. Holding the mule's limp head up, he slashed his throat and stepped back as the blood rushed out of the jugular vein.

His lariat and the man's rope tied to the hind leg, he used the roan to draw the mule up off the ground. At last, with the man's rope tied off, the limp mule swung back and forth off the ground.

"I do not know your name, señor, to properly thank you."

Slocum shook his head as if that was no matter. "Eat the mule. He is a gift and I will pay for the wheel."

"But . . . but, how can I ever repay you?"

"Do a kind thing to another in need."

"I will, señor. I will, señor," he shouted after him.

The awkward woman, on her way with a great knife, stopped to smile up at him. "May Mary, Mother of God, always be with you, señor."

"And with you." He booted the roan on to join the other two.

Theresa smiled when he rode up to her and the Apache sitting their horses.

"I figured you'd not waste them on buzzards," she said and they headed on their way.

"I need to buy a wheel in the next village," Slocum said with a smile for her. "We should be to Alazar by tomorrow night. That's the town in the foothills of the Sierra Madres that trades with broncos. I hope to learn something about Caliche there."

"And the other two mules?" she asked, looking back at the two trailing Domino.

"Oh, we'll find someone needs them by then."

"I bet you do. I bet you do." She laughed aloud.

Slocum found Lopez at his blacksmith shop and dismounted. The man, probably half-black, released the hoof of a horse he was shoeing and straightened to his full six feet tall. "Yes, sah?"

"You Lopez?" Slocum asked.

"Juan Lopez. What you needs?"

"A cart wheel for a friend. He'll be coming after it."

The man folded his arms over his broad chest. "I see."

"He said you wanted two pesos for it."

"That be enough."

"How did you get the name Juan Lopez?" Slocum asked, standing in the stirrups to dig out the money.

"I married me a woman lived down here. I didn't have no name back then, so I took that one." A smile parted his full lips and his dark brown eyes met Slocum's.

"I see." He handed the man the money. "He'll be after it tomorrow."

"No, I's take it out to him and put it on for that much money."

"Good," Slocum said and saluted him before he went to join the others. They rode on.

"He's taking the wheel out and putting it on for them," Slocum said when they wound through the small enclave of jacals under the rustling cottonwoods along the shallow stream. A few cur black dogs barked at them. Several bare-assed, dust-coated kids of both sexes, wearing only ragged short shirts, stood in a row and stared with awed curiosity in their dark eyes at the strangers passing through their small world.

"Bet they'd eat a mule," Theresa said.

He looked over the few women around their adobe shacks busy washing clothes in kettles, who cast suspicious looks at them. With a nod to Theresa, he turned the roan out and took the lead to the red mule from her and promised to catch up with them later.

He jogged the roan back and reined up before Lopez's shed. The big man came outside and put a hand on the post. "You need something else?"

"See this mule?"

"I sees him good. You want to sell him?"

"No." Slocum shook his head and looked the man in the eye. "You never saw him. He's to eat. He gets loose and goes home, he could mean a lot of trouble to you and everyone in this village—you savvy?"

"I savvy." Lopez bobbed his head, then a grin on his full lips showed his white teeth. "We're having a fiesta 'round here."

Slocum nodded.

"Mister," he said with a small grin, "you's always buy wheels for poor folks and gives mules for free away to eat every day?"

"Just on Tuesdays."

"Then I sure be glad you come by today." He laughed and took the mule's lead. "Folks sure going to celebrate around here."

Slocum nodded and reined to leave. The red mule brayed huskily for his ex-companions as Slocum trotted the roan away. Two down, one to go. In the distance he could see the outline of the lofty mother mountains in a purple haze. Somewhere up there, Caliche and his broncos hid from their many enemies. He needed to know what they planned to do next.

6

The one finished bell tower of the Catholic church stuck up on a rise and hovered over Estria. The village was spread along the stream that watered the small fields. This formed a serpentine green belt in the canyon and provided a small-plot agriculture industry that supported the town.

"Where will we stay?" Theresa asked as they went up the sycamore- and cottonwood-lined roadway, dodging *carettas* and small pack trains of burros bristling with firewood sticks.

"Doña DeLong's," Slocum said.

"Who's she?" Theresa looked at the two them for their answer.

"You'll like her," Slocum said and pointed to a two-story house, under a red tile roof on the rise.

"M— What does she do?"

"Her husband once had a gold mine in the Madres."

"He had?"

"Bandits killed him a few years ago in a pack train robbery."

She nodded when he indicated for her to take the drive. They turned off the lane and forded the clear stream, hardly over hock deep on their mounts, and wound their way up to the great house. Dismounted at the hitch rail, Slocum looked up and nodded to the silver-haired, graceful, thin woman who came out of the house and smiled down on them.

"Slocum, I declare. And a lovely woman and your fine scout friend Chako."

48

"Theresa's her name," Slocum said.

"Oh, my dear, welcome to my poor farm."

"I would hardly call it poor," Theresa said and started up the stairs to meet the woman, who held out her arms for her.

"Don't fret over the animals," the doña said to the two men and hugged Theresa. "My dear, you must be exhausted being drug up here over that horrible desert by those two."

"I am fine," Theresa said. "And"—she swung the hair back from her face—"I am so pleased to be here. My, what a lovely farm."

"It needs much work."

"No, it looks like a fairy tale to me. I worked at a mine once and saw a book with pictures. It had a house like this in it."

"My dear, you are delightful. Come along. Estrella has food and that's all men think about—well, when they arrive here anyway."

The two of them laughed privately and went inside the front door. Slocum shook his head and exchanged a look with Chako. "All we get here is food."

"Good food." Chako laughed and rubbed his belly.

With a last glance across the peaceful countryside, Slocum listened to a scolding mockingbird perched in nearby pine, the large brown thrush that mimicked the rest. He heard him. *This may be the Garden of Eden, but it too may have invaders.* Deep in thought about the broncos, he shook his head and followed Chako inside.

Estrella rushed from the kitchen and hugged him. The ample-busted woman smelled of cinnamon and sweets. "So good to have you back. I have a fat lamb in the oven."

"Yes, she said we'll need it today." The doña shook her head. "I said no one was coming. We'd have to eat lamb till we bleated. I should never doubt a *bruja*."

"Not a good one." Slocum squeezed Estrella's shoulder and they exchanged a private look. He never doubted the witches of Mexico. Estrella was a good one.

"Are there men looking for you?" she asked under her breath as if she had discovered something about him.

"You saw them?" he asked.

She nodded. "I will look for their faces and names."

"Do that."

She nodded and then shook hands with Theresa.

"Now, let us freshen, then gather and eat," the doña said, taking charge of the affair.

Slocum went with Chako to wash his hands and face on the back porch. Under the grapevines trellised overhead, Estrella's words came to him. Was Diaz sending more men up his back trail? He hoped not—only time would tell. But he worried more about the other people in that path than himself. Maybe Estrella knew about Caliche too. He'd ask her after the meal.

"I heard her," Chako said, drying his hands and cocking his head to the side in a question for him to answer.

"That some men are looking for me."

The scout looked around to be certain they were alone. "She is a witch. You think she knows?"

"She knew we were coming and cooked a lamb."

The Apache barely nodded his head. He knew all about witches. He agreed.

"Let's eat and then we can visit the cantinas. I need to find out about Caliche and what he will do next."

"If the broncos are close by, I bet I can catch a squaw from his camp coming down here to trade. They can't resist doing that."

"I won't argue with you. You know them."

"I'll find one."

Slocum clapped him on the shoulder as they started inside. "Just be careful that she ain't got a buck shadowing her ass."

"Be careful."

The aroma of the mesquite wood smoke and the richer scent of roasted lamb filled the dining room. Doña DeLong sat at the head and asked Slocum to cut the browned carcass and serve the rest. He set in to cut out the ribeye portions for the two women, then a rack of ribs for his scout and his own plate. Along with steaming rice, frijoles, and sweet peas fresh picked were Estrella's flour tortillas to mop up the rest. Everyone served, he tasted the mild wine, a blush, sipping it for the moisture on his tongue; then he savored a bite of the tender rib meat.

The rich flavor flooded salvia in his mouth. Maybe the doña's house *was* a fairy tale—he damn sure enjoyed it.

After his hot bath and shave, he sat on the porch wrapped in a robe that one of Estrella's helpers had brought him when she came to gather up his clothing in her arms.

"*Mañana*," she said.

"*Sí, mañana. Gracias,*" he said after her, knowing he wouldn't see his clothing until the next day, when she finished with them.

The night sky was sprinkled in stars, and bats swooped around after nocturnal insects. From somewhere nearby, crickets joined the chorus of a million other fiddlers and the soft rush of the stream.

"Where did Chako go?" Theresa asked in a soft voice, coming onto the porch and taking a chair beside him to sit on.

"To look for a squaw. He says they'll come down and trade for things in the village."

"You learn anything in town tonight?"

"Not much. People don't want to talk about trading with the hostiles."

"I bet not. How rich is she?"

"I don't know. Why?"

"This place. All these people that work here."

"Her husband had some gold mines and I think made lots of money in those days before he was killed."

"You went after his killers for her?"

"Yes."

"I understand why she likes you."

"She paid me."

"I don't doubt it. But you are very special to her."

He reached over and clapped his hand on top of hers. "Her husband was a good friend of mine. She didn't have to pay me."

"No one has to pay you. You give money away like water. To—" She lowered her voice. "To whores and beggars and God knows who else."

"Must be why he gives it to me." He leaned over in her face. She met his mouth and kissed him. With a smothered "yes" she turned and put her arms around his neck.

7

Mid-morning the next day, Chako brought back a hellion, gagged, tied, wrapped in a blanket and bound over the back of the mule. The ride back had not taken much of the fight out of her by Slocum's consideration. She twisted and squirmed under the shroud like a muffled wildcat when Chako packed her from the mule to the shed. Amused, Slocum made certain they were alone when he barred the door shut. *Now you've caught her— what the hell are you going to do with her?* This was his man's show, and he was anxious to see what happened next.

"What's her name?"

"Kee." The scout sat astraddle her as he untied the binds that held the blanket around her. Soon two diamond eyes glowered at them like a rattlesnake's as she squirmed and fought against her binds with all her night.

Squatted on his boot heels, Slocum chuckled at Chako's prize. "Be sure she don't bite you when you undo that gag."

Amused, Chako nodded and took off the blanket. Then he jerked her up by the arm, to a sitting position on the dirt. With his finger waving in her face as a warning, he spoke in Apache to her. She made a stone-faced scowl at him, but settled some. Lull before the storm, Slocum considered it. One thing she did not do was agree to Chako's terms.

He undid the gag, but not the ropes. When it was released, she threw her head back and the messed-up long hair flowed back from her face. Slocum guessed her to be in her teens. And definitely an Apache—the centuries of mingling, kidnapping and intermarriage with the Mexican people had brought some beauty to their women in more refined looks.

"Where is Caliche?"

She didn't answer.

"We need to talk to him."

No answer.

"Maybe a couple days tied up in this shed and you will talk to us."

She looked at Slocum and then at Chako. Her words in Apache came hard. Her back stiffened and she sat up straighter.

"She says we should kill her because she will tell us nothing and we should get it over with."

"Tell her that's dumb. Her dead, we'd learn nothing."

"Where is Caliche?"

She shook he head and sulked.

"Get that bottle of whiskey out of my saddlebags." Slocum shifted his weight to his other boot. "We need a party to loosen her up."

Chako grinned and went for it, opening the door and letting sunlight in the shed.

"You are married?" Slocum asked her in Spanish.

"Soldiers killed him."

"Your man is dead?"

She didn't answer. Apaches hated to talk about the dead—considered it caused bad luck.

"You drink whiskey?" he asked her.

"Sometimes."

"Good. We'll get drunk and have a party."

He saw a glint in her eyes that made him think this might suit her—of course, she might also think it was a way to outmaneuver them. Drunk enough, though, she might tell them all they needed to know about the broncos. Chako was back and looking at the label on the bottle of brown liquor in his hand.

"We need some cups."

He handed Slocum the bottle and grinned big. "I go get them."

Slocum cut the seal with his jackknife and looked at her. Then he uncorked the bottle and started to take a sip out of the neck—but paused and met her gaze.

"You want some?" He held the bottle up for her to see it.

Her eyes darted as if to be sure they were alone and then she nodded. He reached over and put the bottle to her lips. Gently he raised it and she took a deep drink. Looking at her closely, he drew the bottle back and watched her swallow. Her eyes watered a little, and a slow smile spread over her coffee-colored face. She nodded for another. He obliged her.

By the time Chako returned with cups, she had taken three big gulps of the whiskey. Her facial expression changed. She looked more interested in the liquor than in "eating them up." Slocum reached behind her and cut her hands free with his jackknife. Rather than rub her red wrists, she reached for the bottle on the ground beside her with both hands and drank a deep one.

"She likes whiskey," Slocum said to Chako, and cut her feet free.

"She really does."

From her throat came a loud "ah" and she smiled foolishly. "Gawdamn good whiskey, you betchem."

She rose and began to hum. Bottle in one hand, she began to stomp her moccasins and chant, "Ho-oh. Hi-oh," going in a circle around the shed's dirt floor. Throwing her head back, she laughed and waved the bottle at them as she went whirling around.

"Didn't need the cups," Chako said and shared a private smile with Slocum.

"I don't think so."

"She really must have drank a lot."

"On an empty stomach it works faster." Slocum watched her stomp around in a big circle.

"Oh, yes."

When she came by, Slocum snatched the whiskey bottle from her. "You good woman." He winked at her and took a small sip, making a big deal of it.

"Gawd—damn—right—goo-woman." She slapped him on

the chest with an open hand and weaved. She fought with the ties on her skirt. Then she had them loose and stepped out of it. Her brown legs flashed in the shed's light shafts.

"You like pussy?" she slurred.

"Bet you have a good one."

She nodded and reached for the bottle, but he held it far enough back that she couldn't reach it. "Where's Caliche?"

Like she'd never heard that before, she blinked at him. "In the mountains—jacking off, huh?"

"He going to raid San Carlos?"

"No guns. No ammo." She pulled on his arm for the bottle. "Sumbitch—no bullets him says."

"He going to buy some?"

She stopped reaching for the bottle, pressed one hard breast into him and ran her right hand over the mound in his pants. "I give you big fuck for bottle."

He ignored her approach. "Is someone bringing him guns and ammo?"

Looking groggily up at him, she mumbled, "Slade bring guns."

"This side or that of the border?"

She shook her head. "Him . . . maybe . . . send . . . word."

"That son of a bitch—"

"You got more gawdamn whiskey?" she asked.

"Bottles of it."

"Good. I need lots and lots."

"I'll give you a mule to ride back. Don't tell anyone about this."

She ran her hands down the tops of her legs, then looked up at him through the tangled hair in her face. "For a mule I won't tell anyone."

He looked over at Chako squatted by the door. "Slade is supposed to be getting guns for them."

"What we do?"

"For my money, you can go find that other bottle of whiskey and have a stomp with her."

Chako grinned.

"Give her that third mule too."

"Okay. Maybe I can learn more from her."

"Do it." Slocum laughed and headed for the main house. Needed to get the colonel word to be on the lookout for those two. Of course, they'd broken out of the jail in Tucson and sure needed to make some money to escape the territory. Those women and the wagons might be the key. Perhaps in the morning he'd send Chako back to Bowie.

When Slocum crossed the fields headed for the big house, he saw no one working in the garden and wondered for a moment where they were. Taking a siesta? He checked the sun time. Not lunchtime yet. Then he saw a hip-shot horse, white with dried salt and trail dust, hitched near the barn. Who owned that pony?

Keeping in the cover of some apple trees, he squatted down to appraise the situation. How many more rode-hard horses were in there? He could hear others coughing and blowing. That answered his question. More than one. Their mounts partially secluded, no doubt they either held the house or had it covered.

He hurried   d got Don Torrez and his vaqueros at the corral with a finger to is mouth for silence. "Bandits are around the house. Be careful for the women. They are killers." He sent them in a circle around the structure.

Then he opened the shed door and disturbed Chako's seduction of the squaw. "Bandits," he hissed, "all around the house."

Disengaging himself, Chako nodded, grabbed up his six-gun with a nod and grinned.

In matter of minutes, with only three shots fired, the invaders were either dead or bound prisoners. The women were fine and Slocum reassured them that the raid had been thwarted.

A half hour later, a council was held by the men at the corrals—the silver-headed Segundo Don Torrez, two of Doña's vaqueros plus Chako and Slocum.

"The ones we have that are alive will only ride back to this *general* and bring back more," Don Torrez said. His vaqueros nodded their sombreros as if in deep concentration over the matter.

"So what do we do?" Slocum asked. "The officials here will do nothing to them in fear the *general* will take his revenge out on the village."

The older of the two vaqueros slid his brown hand flat over his throat in a sign. "Then we bury them and take their horses up in the canyon and do the same to them for the buzzards."

"I hate that they came here after me."

"No," the don said. "These hombres came here to hurt our guests. We will handle them. No one will know."

"I must take word north in the morning."

"We will be fine," the don said, and his two men agreed with solemn nods. "Thanks for saving our doña."

8

Slocum and Chako headed north in the predawn. Theresa agreed to stay with Doña DeLong and look after her—besides, this would be a hard, quick trip back to Bowie. Slocum didn't trust the telegraph—in the first place the Mexican connection was undependable, and secondly one could never be certain the message would even get through. Letters were sometimes faster.

The open desert country between there and the border was mostly greasewood-clad alkali country—little water and most of it gyp. Before they left that morning, Don Torrez said that the matter of the *general*'s men and their horses had been handled. Theresa thanked Slocum; she was pleased he had found her such a grand place and he should come back to see her when he could. He agreed and kissed her good-bye.

"We should make the springs at Aqua Fria by late tonight," Chako said as they hard-trotted their rested mounts.

"Good. We can catch a little sleep there and then push on." Slocum wanted to be in Bowie in two days' travel. He didn't want Slade headed south with any guns and ammo for the broncos—it would only encourage them to raid back across the border. Also, a show of ammo and new guns might encourage more young bucks at San Carlos to join him.

"What's this Caliche like? I never met him."

"He is a *brujo*. If you entered the Madres today, he would have a vision of your coming."

58

"How?" Slocum blinked his dry eyes. What was this man?

"How do such things work?" Chako shrugged under the faded army shirt as they rode. "Once he said after a dream, three men would ride up this canyon and have their saddlebags full of gold coins."

Slocum nodded and looked ahead at the wavering heat rising off the desert and distorting the faraway saw-topped mountains. The bronco leader must have powers that enforced his leadership. Visionaries always impress Stone Age people, and even some that weren't from that era.

"Those men came that day up that canyon and his men ambushed them. They had much new money."

"Is that why they go to him?"

"What else do they know to do? The army says they can't raid the Mexicans, Papagos or Pimas anymore. They can't drink *tiswain* or beat their wives. What else can an Apache do? Farm? That is women's work—besides, there is little farmland at San Carlos to plow and water."

"Wish I had a vision about him."

"Like what?"

"A vision of when he plans to leave those mountains and go for the guns."

Chako nodded. "Maybe we should ask a *bruja*?"

"I asked Estrella and she shook her head."

"I know an old woman who could tell you, but she is in the White Mountains."

"Who's she?"

"My grandmother."

"Maybe we need to talk to her."

"Maybe."

Long past dark they reached the small village of Aqua Fria and watered their horses at the well in the small square. A few tall palms rose into the starry night above them. Lights were still on in the cantina. After washing his hands and face in the tank, Slocum motioned his head in that direction and Chako agreed. They led their mounts over there and hitched them.

The rotund bartender with a rag over his arm came and took

their order for some food and a bottle of mescal to wash down the trail dust.

"The goat—he is fresh cooked. A milk-fat one too."

"Good," Slocum said and they sipped the sharp mescal out of tin cups until an ample-bodied short woman, with deep cleavage exposed, delivered their food on a large platter. She smiled and laughed freely.

"Ah, such *grandes hombres*—why you ride so late in the night?"

"To get here and feel you," Slocum said and reached out to familiarly rub her butt with his palm while she served them on plates. Nothing under the thin skirt except her hard ass. She moved closer to him.

"Your amigo, he is a *grande gringo*," she said with a grin to Chako and handed him a plate of the browned goat meat, black beans and corn tortillas.

"*Mucho grande*." Chako smiled big at her.

When she put Slocum's plate before him, she slid onto the bench beside him. "I will feed you."

"Oh, I am much to tired to make love to you. You will forgive me," he said, diving into his food and ignoring her closeness. Morning would come in four hours, and they needed to be in the saddle and gone.

"Oh, men," she said and stomped off.

"Get me up before sunup," he said to Chako and shook his head in disbelief that he'd turned her down.

Chako was there before the rooster crowed with their horses, crouched in the predawn shadows nearby as the horses' soft coughing awoke Slocum. He got out of his bedroll to dress. It would be a long ride ahead and a hard push to ever reach Bowie, but they'd try. Dressed and in the saddle in minutes, they were gone. No hot coffee, no breakfast—his dry mouth tasted like ten Apaches warriors had trod through it barefooted all night, he really felt downcast. He pushed Roan hard northward—they had business in Bowie.

Long past midnight, on borrowed horses, they reached the springs below Bowie and fell from the saddle like stunned men. Slocum looked at the peak above them under the quarter moon and shook his head. "The old man's asleep. I'll see him in the morning. Where're you going?"

"Get some food." Chako went off in the night.

"You don't like my jerky—" Slocum shook his head and pulled loose the sweat-soaked latigos. "Old pony, I'll feed you in the daylight."

The saddle off the horse, he shook all over, then dropped to his front knees to roll in the sandy wash bed. Slocum let him, and undid the strings on his blanket roll. That spread out, he hobbled the horse, who was back on his feet. Then, too stupid-tired to do more, he took off his gun belt, lay down and went to sleep.

After daybreak, he was up at headquarters and met Captain Moore behind the desk. "Morning. Where's the colonel?"

"Thought you were in Mexico."

"I was two days ago. He here?"

"Colonel, Slocum's here to see you," Moore called out over his shoulder to the open door behind him.

"Send him in."

"Go ahead."

"Good morning—" Woolard peered hard at him. "Man, you look tough."

"Tough is good word for it. That's not the problem. Slade is getting guns for the broncos. He needs to be stopped."

"Where? How?"

"I'm not certain, but the word's good. Caliche has enough money or gold to buy whatever Slade can get through."

"What do we need to do?"

"Patrol south of the Muleshoes to the Peralta Springs. I feel sure Slade will use the east side of the territory to slip down there."

"Guess you didn't learn anything about that Mexican bandit?"

"We did," Slocum said and told him the story of the horse raid and the incident in the foothills.

The Colonel's blue eyes twinkled with amusement. "Word was out that someone had sent a herd of rustled horses into the old man's place and no one would figure out who did it or why."

"They thought it was a raid and probably shot a few of the horses before they figured it out."

"What can we do about this *general*?"

"He's tough," Slocum began and told him about the incident at Doña DeLong's casa.

"We need to coax him up here and ambush him." The colonel looked out the small four-pane window at the parade ground. "You know the U.S. could have bought that whole northern third of Mexico when they made the Gadsden Purchase—damn. If they had, we'd be in charge and the Apaches couldn't run and hide from us."

"Nor could the ten-cent bandits."

"Right. All Congress wanted was a strip of land down here to put the year-round southern railroad through. Well, they goofed." The major shook his head. "Where are you going?"

"Tucson and see if Slade's getting his guns there."

"Good, idea. Be careful."

"I will."

"Slocum—that schoolmarm you rescued asked about you at the dance last Friday."

"Oh."

The major grinned. "She's lovely. The officers like to have danced her to death, I thought."

Slocum shook his head. "She's tougher than you might imagine."

"A very grand young lady. I'll have the patrols and more scouts out looking for them. You get me any word that will help."

"I will, sir. I'm going to buy two new horses in Tucson and charge them to the quartermaster. I ran my good roan into the ground getting back here and so did Chako. Horses we have, we borrowed."

"I'll handle it. You taking the stage over there?"

"Yes, to Tucson. We'll need transportation to Bowie. Chako's arranging to send the horses we borrowed back."

"Fine. Captain Moore, get him two passes for the stage to Tucson. He'll need a transport to Bowie later."

"One o'clock," Slocum said and started to leave.

"The ride will be hitched and ready," Moore said.

"Thanks, and I'll let you know what I find."

"Good. Where to now?" Woolard asked.

"A bath, a shave and clean clothes."

Woolard nodded, smiled and waved him on. "Thanks. You are my eyes and ears out there."

He took his shave and bath from a washerwoman known as Big Madge and learned from her that Clanton had the rifles for the gunrunners. After a good night's sleep, he stopped by and told Woolard about Clanton and the rifles. His response came with a scowl.

"Damn, that sumbitch. But—but how did you learn that on this base?"

"Birds talk to me."

Woolard gave him a look of disbelief. "We'll put a lookout for that too."

"Good. I'm off to Tucson."

"You know, Clanton finds out you're working against him, you can chalk up another name on that list of them out to get you."

"Colonel, they won't none get a cherry."

Woolard laughed and waved him on.

The ride to Bowie with Chako in the ambulance was rough and dusty. The stage line had switched to the small towns rather than using Apache Pass. This would someday be the route of the Southern Pacific if they ever got their money situation straightened out. The track ended at Deming, New Mexico, over a hundred miles east, and nothing had been laid in nine months.

They unloaded their saddles and gear on the boardwalk and Slocum thanked the corporal and his man before they pulled out. Slocum brushed off his front and told Chako he'd be back. He stuck his head in the stage office, and the telegraph operator under the celluloid nodded.

"Stage on time?"

"Be close. Due here at seven."

"I have two passes."

The man nodded his approval. "There will be seats."

Slocum entered the grocery/mercantile and saw the golden

hair he recalled walking past him that morning in the desert. Mary Harbor, with her face washed and in clean clothes, shone like a diamond among the piles of merchandise on the counters.

"Why, Slocum, you're back," she said, and the glint in her blue eyes raised his temperature a notch.

"How are things going?" he asked, removing his hat for her.

"School? Oh, fine. The children speak mostly Spanish, but we are both learning."

"Must be a challenge."

"Oh, it is, but I love them."

"I'm catching a stage in a few hours and thought I'd drop by and see how you were doing. Sounds good."

"Well, we could stroll the block of boardwalk if you'd like," she said. The lilt in her voice raised his spirits.

"Let's," he said and used his hat to show her the way ahead of him to the front door.

"What have you been doing?"

"Oh, just scouting."

"Like the day you found me?"

He carefully searched the street for any sign, replaced his hat and then nodded. "Not too exciting."

"Oh, I would think it could be. The Apaches sound unsettled." She put her hand in the crook of his and they went up the boardwalk.

"Anyone who had to live at San Carlos would rather be dead than there."

"Bad place?"

"Excuse me but I consider the place hell. Those people lived in the mountains—they've never been farmers, not to any degree."

"What should be done for them?"

"I'm not sure. Too many bad deals've been made now to go back." He shook his head in surrender.

"Let me show you my school," she said, taking him on the path through the tall greasewood. The narrow pathway led down into a dry wash and up the bank. A hot wind swept his face when he looked back to be certain they were alone. Soon they came to a cleared spot, and an adobe building sat in the matted dry grass, a plain-looking flat-roofed structure that acted like an elixir for her when she led him to the front door.

"Close your eyes."

He obeyed her and she opened the door. "Now look."

The wall he faced had a mural started on it of a bigger-than-life scene with brown-skinned children dancing around the building. She pointed to the unfinished sketch of a barrel cactus, leaning as they did toward the sun.

"I wanted one in it."

"Who is doing this?"

"Oh, the children. They are very talented."

"It looks so well done—"

She threw her arms around him and laid her face on his shirtfront. "Oh, I couldn't leave them. They are so talented and—I am shameless, because I prayed you'd come back and hold me."

He laid his cheek on the top of her head and smelled the freshness of her hair. "I'm a poor one to wait on."

"Just allow me that luxury."

"I don't want to destroy your reputation."

She threw her head back and looked him in the face. "Ruin it. I double dare you."

His mouth closed on hers, and he tasted the honey of her lips as he squeezed her tight to his body. The lithe, firm form of her against his own drove lightning through his veins until at last he raised his face away and looked into the blue pools. "My God, girl, you're serious."

"Shamelessly." She drove her breasts into him and squeezed him tight.

"Not here. Not now. I'll be back."

"Promise?"

"Promise."

"Good. I can wait, but not forever."

An hour later, wedged in the rocking couch seat with Chako and some whiskey-stinking drummer, he still could smell her in his nostrils and taste her on his tongue. *Damn you, Mary Harbor, I'll be thinking about you all the way there and back.*

9

Tucson was a place where they found a dead donkey lying in a pothole beside the boardwalk. His carcass fed the many vultures perched all around on the trees and jacal roofs, as well as a dozen cur dogs fighting over his intestines in the lamplight escaping from the saloon's front doors. This was no fresh death. It was over a week since the donkey's expiration and it reeked in putrefaction's arms—which did not lessen the enthusiasm of the curs or the big birds in the daytime consumption of the remains.

His saddle on his shoulder, Slocum and his likewise burdened scout headed for Pearson's Livery, a half block away in the starry night. They found bunks and slept until sunup. After breakfast in a small café, they went back to find new horses.

Livery owner Rube Pearson spat tobacco in the middle of most of his sentences. "I've got some"—spit—"of the best horses in the territory." He indicated the pen full of horses and mules.

"Highest priced too," Slocum said.

"Yeah, but that damn army"—spit—"won't pay me for six months or longer."

"You couldn't make that much interest on your money in a bank."

"Bank?" Pearson spat aside and wiped his mouth on the back of his hand. "I don't ever use a damn bank."

Slocum nodded and picked out a leggy bay horse that looked sound and who mouthed as a four-year-old. Chako found a bald-faced sorrel that struck his fancy. Small, but it fit the Apache, plus it was flashy. Saddles cinched on their purchases, they left Pearson spitting and sputtering how hard it was to collect off the army quartermaster.

"Where we going?" Chako asked when they were in the saddle.

"I figure we can't learn much till dark in town," Slocum said as he reined his gelding around a burro train, each one stacked high with firewood sticks and branches. "We'll go out to Rensoe's until then."

Manchew Rensoe's place was on the Santa Cruz River, and the green fields of alfalfa and corn shone in the bright sun. When they rode up to the recently white-plastered casa, a great barrel-chested man with a black beard came out and blinked at them against the morning sun's glare.

"That you, Slocum?"

"No, I'm a traveling brush salesman. How you been, *mi amigo*?" he asked, stepping off the horse.

Rushing out to grasp his hand in both of his, the big man soon hugged him and pounded him on the back. "Good to see you, *mi amigo*. Where you been? Screwing all the sweet pussy in Sonora?"

Slocum shook his head. "I left plenty for you. This is Chako."

"Ah, Chako, you must have fun riding with him, no?"

The Apache shook his hand and nodded. "Big-time. He knows lots of women."

"Ah, *sí*, he is a bad hombre. Why are you here?"

"We need to rest today and go into Tucson tonight. Jed Slade is trying to get guns to sell to the broncos."

"Didn't he break out of jail?"

"He didn't go far, I'd bet good money."

"Not if it would make that Tucson Ring any money. Those bastards are robbing the government at every corner and inciting the broncos on the other side. Come on the porch—Juanita, bring us something cool." He led the way to the palm-frond-shaded patio on the side of the house and showed them chairs. "This Slade is a weasel. A two-bit thief and whiskey runner. I don't doubt he bribed the jailer and got out."

"Probably, but we've got more troubles. We know that Caliche has the gold to pay him."

"What happened to the damn Indians? They used to say put the gold back."

"Now they know it buys things like guns." Chako laughed aloud.

"*Carumba!* They know that now?" Rensoe slapped his forehead with his palm.

Amused, Chako nodded.

"So no word of him or his partner Thorpe?" Slocum asked.

"Not a word." Rensoe shook his head and replaced the curly strands with his palm. With a scowl he cut his dark gaze around, looking for her. "Where is that woman?"

Slocum shook his head, having no idea. "They had some women and a wagon with oxen up there east of the Dos Cabasos and Bowie. I figure they had time to get down here since then."

"Good-looking women?" Rensoe's white teeth gleamed behind his copper lips.

"Not bad," Slocum said and his scout nodded in agreement. "We didn't have time for them. The army's been running our butts off. We've been to the base of the Madres and back in a week."

"Damn, they have been working you too hard—ah, about time. Where have you been?" Rensoe said to the dark-skinned woman delivering a tray and glasses.

"I was busy," she said to him as haughtily as she could manage and set the tray down.

He slapped her hard on the butt with the palm of his hand. "Next time move faster."

"Next time maybe I kill you," she said and used her index finger in Rensoe's face to punctuate her words. With her other hand, she rubbed her butt as if the blow had hurt her.

"Ha," he said and reached to pour wine in their glasses. "These are important men who come to see me. You leave them thinking we have poor service here."

"I have some *cabrito* ready, you want some to feed them."

He nodded. "They would eat some young goat cooked over the mesquite slow, huh?"

"Sure," Slocum said and his scout agreed.

"I will bring it in a few minutes," she said as if to warn Rensoe it would not be *mucho pronto*.

They drank his good wine and ate the tangy meat, with roasted sweet and hot peppers, mashed frijoles and spicy rice all wrapped in her fresh-made flour tortillas. The rich food drew the saliva in Slocum's mouth, and they both ate until they were too full. Their host then showed them to some shaded hammocks for a siesta and excused himself. He promised to wake them for supper; after that they could ease back into the *barrio* and look for information about the pair of escapees.

Slocum closed his eyes and thought about Mary Harbor. He dreamed about her dancing for him wearing a filmy dress of veils in a room of flickering candles. Her golden hair was piled high with pins, and he watched the curve of her slender neck, wishing to reach out and cradle it in his hands. To lift her face up and kiss her sweet lips while she scrambled naked underneath him; to slide his turgid dick tight in her grasp against her shield. Then his hips moved forward with the head of it poised against the restriction—

"Hombre, wake up, I have news." Rensoe was shaking him.

Bleary-eyed and in a sweat, Slocum sat upright. "Damn, I was sure dreamin'."

"Sorry, but I have word those women are out by the fort."

"How?"

"I spoke to an amigo who came by, and he told me that those women were camped east of Fort Thomas on the creek."

"Good." Slocum slung on his right boot sitting on the edge of the hammock. "Those two devils may be out there too, hanging around them. Your friend say what they were doing out there?"

"Whoring around."

Slocum nodded. "They might be good at that."

Chako nodded and grinned. "I want the one with the titties."

"Huh?" Rensoe asked with a frown.

Seated on the hammock, Slocum dumped his boot to be certain no vermin had crawled in and looked up at their host. "Those girls were ready to trade pussy for the release of them two. And I made them take off the clothing they'd stolen, so we saw all of them. I mean all of them."

"Who are they?"

"One is Slade's woman—wife? The other is Thorpe's wife and daughters, I'd guess."

"The girls weren't bad-looking," Chako said and stretched his arms over his head then yawned. "I'd've fucked them, then took those two in anyway." The Apache laughed and so did Slocum and Rensoe.

"We were in a hurry. Next time we'll do that," Slocum promised.

Chako shrugged like it didn't matter and went for the horses.

"You think you'll find those two gun runners?"

"We need to. General Crook's unhappy. He's coming down from Prescott to take charge of this campaign, I figure."

"Hell, it's nice and cool up there at Prescott. Bowie is a hothouse compared to that high country."

"Yes, but there ain't been any results in a long while on rounding them up. I'm sure Sherman is eating his ass out over getting some results for all the monies being spent down here."

"Hell, Tucson would dry up and blow away without all the money the Apache business pumps into the Ring."

Slocum nodded. "Them and old man Clanton live high on the hog on it."

"Stealing cattle in Mexico to sell to the U.S. government— fine contractors, huh?"

"The best that bribery and under-the-table deals can find. All they do is overcharge and bitch about how long it takes for their payment to get there."

"Where do you want to meet tonight?" Rensoe asked when Chako led up the horses.

"Saguaro Cantina"

Rensoe nodded and then grinned big. "Don't get any cholla needles in your dick out there screwing them whores."

"I'll be careful."

"Good—tonight at the cantina."

Slocum agreed and took the reins. They rode out to Fort Thomas, and Chako learned from another Apache scout where the women were camped up the almost dry creek bed. They rode around the adobe barracks and up the water course's sandy bottom without any more contact with other scouts or the military. Their presence was noted with a nod from some enlisted men, but they rode on.

The sun was burning up the daylight in a final blazing sunset. They smelled campfire smoke and dismounted. Their horses hitched to some mesquites in a draw, they went on foot to spy on the camp. In the dim twilight, Slocum could make out the cob-pipe-smoking Mother Thorpe giving orders to the others in the firelight. He counted two of the girls and not the taller Sadie. They squatted on their boot heels and watched for any signs of the last one.

"Slade's woman Sadie ain't there," Slocum said in a guarded voice.

"Figure she's with him?" Chako asked.

"Or she's working on her back."

Chako nodded and grinned. "I want the one with the pointed titties."

"Candy."

The scout agreed with a bob of his head.

"We better locate Slade's woman if we can."

"You stay here. I go find her."

At Slocum's nod, the Apache slipped off into the growing darkness. If she was close by, Chako would find her, and much quicker than he could. All he could do was wait and listen to the locusts' creak in the night.

A man rode up on horseback, and Slocum could see by his shape that it wasn't Slade or Thorpe. He laughed loud, and his booming voice carried. "I come for me some."

The words of Mother Thorpe were too low for Slocum to hear.

"Hell, yes, I've got the money. Show me the merchandise, woman."

Mother Thorpe's hand was held out for the money, and Slocum could see the two younger girls lined up in the fire's light for the bearded man's approval.

"How much for both of them?" he roared. Then he shouted, "By grab, I'll take both of them."

Mother Thorpe shook her head in disgust, and the three of

them climbed in the back of the covered wagon. The last Slocum saw of them, the man was feeling the final girl's ass real familiar-like as they disappeared.

Chako, with a grin, returned and shook his head. "She not there."

"She's probably with Slade and Thorpe. Wonder where they're hiding."

The scout shook his head.

"We might just as well get back to Tucson and meet Rensoe. Besides old Whiskers in there has the pointed tit one and her sister busy right now anyway."

"Who is he?"

"I have no idea, but he's either full of wind or horny as hell."

"I heard his voice before." Chako shook his head. "Don't remember where."

"Tell me if you remember. Wonder where them two are hiding."

"Not close to here."

"I know. Let's go see what we can learn in town."

They mounted up and rode back. Long past sundown, they rode up the dark, shadowy streets, striped by lights from open doors and noisy cantinas. Finding a place at the crowded hitch rack, they tied their horses and went inside the smoky interior. Rensoe was in a booth by himself and they joined him.

"Learn anything?"

"Slade's wife Sadie isn't out there, and the men ain't around. Thorpe's wife and his daughters are running a whorehouse in the covered wagon."

"Low rent," Rensoe said and laughed. "I sent for the guy that may know."

Slocum nodded and ordered two beers from the skinny barmaid standing above him and busy scratching her hip through the dress. "I don't serve Injuns."

"He ain't Indian, he's a damn Mexican," Slocum said. "Get you ass over there and get me two beers."

"Yah, yah, he's Mexican, all right."

Rensoe shook his head in disgust after her. "Juarez will be here in a little while."

"What will he know?" Slocum asked, appraising the tough crowd lounging at the crowded bar or playing cards at the tables. The yellow light from the overhead lamps, fogged with the smoke, cast everything in the room in browns and grays.

She brought the two beers and stood hipshot while he dug out the change to pay her. With a scowl at the three dimes he put in her hand, she went sashaying her slutty ass off to wait on others.

"Maybe she thought you owed her lots of money." Rensoe laughed.

Slocum shook his head to dismiss the thought of the ugly woman. "Bet that dime's her biggest tip tonight,"

They all three chuckled.

A short, handsome Mexican with a bright smile crossed the room and nodded to them.

"Juarez, these are *mi amigos*," Rensoe said and indicated them. "Those two gringos broke out of jail a week or so ago—where are they?"

"At a ranchería north of the Santa Catalinas."

"Can you show them that place tomorrow?"

The man in his thirties looked pained. "My horse, he's not so good."

"They'll bring you one that's good."

Slocum nodded.

"Sure—my house. What time?"

"Sunup?" Slocum asked and Juarez agreed.

Rensoe clapped him on the arm. "They will pay you well, and thank you, my friend."

A broad smile, a nod, and Juarez was gone.

"Well, I bet you find the woman there too."

Chako curled his lip. "She's the ugly one."

They laughed. Slocum felt better. Perhaps before another sun went down they'd have those two arrested again. Then he could worry about Diaz and the broncos down in the Madres. What was Mary Harbor doing? She was hard to clear out of his mind.

"You and that Messikin want another beer?" The barmaid broke into his thoughts, standing there scratching,

"Bring three," he said and smiled at her.

10

"Day late and a dollar short.' Slocum shook his head in disgust when they found the camp behind the Catalinas empty. "Well, you can tell your amigo, Juarez, that he can use this jacal now for his sheepherder." He dropped out of the saddle and undid the girth. *Those two slipped away again.* That was sure unhandy; he and Chako needed to be back in Sonora checking on the broncos and what mischief Diaz was into. He scrubbed his beard-stubble-edged mouth with his callused palm. Nothing they could do here.

"Which way did they go?"

"Toward the mountains."

Slocum threw his head back to study the towering range. Strange they would go that way. But they might have another hideout up there too. They obviously were elusive, or else law, the sheriff or U.S. deputy marshals would have found them.

"Should we follow them?" Chako asked with a head toss to the mountains.

"No, we've wasted enough time. They're on the move. They probably realized when that goat man came by that he'd spread the word. He's real lucky they didn't kill him."

Juarez agreed with smile. "He's very lucky."

They rode back to Tucson, arriving after sundown at Rensoe's. He came out to greet them.

"You did no good, *mi amigo*?"

74

Slocum shook his head. "They moved off, probably about the time the goat man found them."

"What now?"

"We head back to Bowie, I guess. Woolard needs some more reports out of Mexico on Diaz and the broncos."

"I'm sorry."

"No need. I paid Juarez ten pesos for his troubles and he went home. Guess we ought to try and squeeze some information out of Thorpe's whores, but they probably don't know anything either."

Rensoe agreed. "Come have some wine and some food. You two must be starved."

Chako grinned big with his saddle in his hands. "We can eat, huh?"

"Sure. Why?"

"I thought Slocum was going to starve me to death."

The three laughed.

"Ah, Juanita," Rensoe said, hugging the swarthy-faced woman around the shoulders when they reached the patio. "Our guests have returned."

"And hungry, I suppose?" Her thick eyebrows cocked in a frown.

"Ah, you are so perceptive, my sweet one."

"I know you so well."

"Did your friends arrive?" He looked back at the lighted doorway.

"Yes."

"Perhaps they would like to meet *mi amigos*." Rensoe showed Slocum and Chako to the chairs. "A widow woman and her daughter are here from Tubac. Her husband was killed by the Apaches a few months ago."

"Perhaps," Juanita said. "I will ask them."

"Good. Bring us some wine now."

"*Sí.*" She whirled and went back inside.

Rensoe looked back at the doorway then turned and grinned. "Wait till you see Doña Malone. She is a very pretty woman." He made a circle with his forefinger and thumb. "Mucho pretty."

Juanita brought the wine and the cups, set them on the table and nodded as if to say, *Are you satisfied?* to her man. There was talk inside, and the laughter of women carried onto the porch as they sipped on the rich wine. Slocum had begun to feel a little sleepy gazing at the stars overhead.

"I am going to open my mine in Madeira Canyon again," Rensoe said. "Besides, I can use the money. It is far enough away from the Apaches, I think I can operate it without so many guards."

Slocum nodded. "That should work. Just keep an eye out for bandits. They still filter across the border."

"Oh, I'll hire enough—but I won't need a damn army like a few years ago."

The three women came out then and delivered the food. Slocum saw the beauty in the woman instantly—Doña Malone was a very attractive woman even dressed in black. The other girl must be her daughter, he decided.

"Ah, Doña Malone, this is *mi amigo* Slocum." Rensoe scrambled to get up.

"So nice to meet you," Slocum said, removing his hat and accepting her smooth hand in his. He looked deep into the pools of liquid brown and then kissed her hand.

"Señor Slocum," she said in a smoky voice. "So nice to meet you. My daughter Avonna."

"That is my scout Chako Smith," he said as the teenage girl curtsied for him.

The sly smile on Avonna's face almost said, *My, what a neat-looking Apache*. Slocum showed the doña to a chair and took a seat beside her.

"You live in Tubac?"

"Close by there. But I am trying to sell our *rancheria*." She used the back of her hand to sweep the long hair back from her face. "It is hard to keep help. They don't like working for a woman is what it is. The rustlers have struck twice. So I guess I need to sell and move to Tucson."

"You have help now?"

"*Amor*—Rensoe has found me a few good vaqueros. It is better, and they are very respectful." She shook her head as if upset.

"You had trouble with help before?"

"Yes," she said in a low voice. Her eyes darted around to be certain the others were beyond earshot. "Those men who used to work for me—they raped my poor daughter and me."

Slocum frowned. "The law do anything?"

She shrugged. "It would be my word against them."

"Who were they?"

Her thick, long lashes wet, she shook her head. About to cry, she rose and ran away down the hall. Slocum looked after her and shook his head.

"What is wrong with her, *mi amigo*?" Rensoe asked with his hands full of tortillas and food.

"I think she had some grief get after her."

"Don't be upset, señor. My mother cries very easy these days," Avonna, her daughter, said and went back to talking to Chako between bites.

"I better go see about her," Slocum said.

Rensoe nodded. "Maybe you can comfort her. She is in the third bedroom."

"I'll find her."

"Ah, *sí*, and you bring her back and eat."

"I'll try."

Slocum hurried down the dimly lighted hallway and rapped on the door.

"Go away."

"You know sometimes it helps to talk about things."

"Not this—it won't bring him back—won't fix a thing . . ."

He tried the knob and the door came open. She turned from the star-lighted patio door and looked at him so sadly, it gnawed at his guts. Filled with a need to revenge her disgrace, he crossed the tile floor to her. In a smooth effort, he swept her up in his arms and lifted her high enough that they were face to face. In her eyes he saw all the agony, the shame and the hurting. Their mouths touched and her arms flew around his neck.

When at last they broke for air, he backed up enough to drop his butt on the bed with her in his lap. "Sorry I smell like a horse and need a shave."

"No, you are exactly like my husband when he returned

from roundup." She threw her hair back then nestled in his arms. "He always was hungry when he came back—and not for food either."

He nodded. "Not for food."

"We will be missed." She motioned toward the front of the house.

"It is only your reputation that concerns me."

"Ha, what is that?"

"I'll have to ride on come the dawn."

She nodded and began to unbutton his shirt. "Only if you make me forget."

"And if I don't?"

"Then you must stay until you do."

He gave a short chuckle. "That sounds serious."

The moisture on her eyelids danced like diamonds in the pearl light invading the room. She looked up at him. "Just don't tell me I am a fool."

He squeezed her tightly in his arms. "No, my lovely lady, you could never be a fool."

11

Slocum and Chako rode part of the way back to Bowie the next day. His concern was about them ever finding suitable horses to ride in the Bowie region, since the broncos had rustled so many that good horses brought as much as two-fifty at Tombstone. With the sweet perfume taste of Doña Malone still in his nostrils and on his tongue, and the memory of her wild ways riding on his mind, he felt hungover. Damn, what a night. He peeked out from under the stiff brim of his four-corners hat and checked the mid-afternoon sun time.

"We make Benson by night, I'll be pleased," he said as they trotted their horses down the stage road. The stakes for the future railroad were on the right-of-way a hundred yards beyond their route. "That girl ever tell you those rannies' names that raped those two?"

Chako nodded. "Whitey Blaines, Curly France and Elliot."

"Must have been bad."

"I think so. She said they tied them both up naked on her mother's bed and took turns trying to fuck them, and they were real drunk."

"Trying?" Slocum blinked at him.

"Yeah, she laughed and said they weren't much good at it either. Their dicks never got very hard. But I knew it was not funny to her, I mean why she laughed."

"I understand. How long did all this last?"

79

"Couple of days."

"Oh. No wonder her mother was so upset." Slocum gave a shudder of his shoulders and looked off at the purple Rincon Mountains. Those three bastards needed to be taught a lesson.

"Avonna thinks them cowboys went to work for old man Clanton after they left them."

"Good. We may meet those sonsabitches someday."

"I'm ready."

"Let's lope some. We need to make the Cienga station by sundown."

Chako nodded and they set out.

Past noon the next day, Slocum reported to Woolard. In a chair facing the colonel's large desk, he sat in the hot office with little breeze coming in the open doors and windows, and they discussed the effort to locate the gunrunners.

"Well, I agree it's best you came back. Crook is getting ready to take several companies across the border. The Mexicans can't make up their minds about how many they will allow in."

"We'll head south. I'm not too sure that Slade and Thorpe can raise the money to buy those arms in the first place. Being on the run and all. And if I know him, the old man ain't taking any credit I bet from those two."

"They might not live to come back and pay him, huh?"

"Exactly, plus some bandit general like Diaz might be waiting for them to come back."

Woolard scowled. "He's as much a pain in the ass as the broncos these days. Wells Fargo is quite certain he held up the stage between the border and Benson carrying gold from a Mexican mine. And unlike the Apaches, the Mexican authorities sure won't let you chase him down in Mexico."

"No. He's making himself a name as sort of a Robin Hood too with giving out some things to the peons."

"That doesn't surprise me. Probably stuff he stole in his raids. Always easy to give away something that cheap. So far he's eluded the patrols we have on the border in his coming and goings." Woolard shook his head. "You figure out a good plan to get him, let me know. I'm just dreading Crook coming here and heading this invasionary force."

"Why is that?" Slocum sat back and tented his fingers to touch his nose.

"Nothing anyone does will please him. We are short way too many cav horses. A dismounted cavalry is like a sore-toed bear—mad all the time. There are not enough conveyances to get them down there—so we are not highly mobile." Woolard made a wry scowl of distaste. "And those damn vast Sierra Madres are over a hundred miles away. More like one fifty."

"Good luck. Chako and I'll go back and see what we can learn."

"Oh, Ike had a big horse sale at Charleston—those horses you sent him sold well."

"I bet they did."

"My quartermaster went, but said they exceeded the price that he could pay."

"I never figured that they'd make the old man rich, but he's made lots of money off the U.S. Army and the Indian agencies."

"Thousands of dollars." Woolard rose and paced the floor. "Crook will sure be upset. But that's not your worry. I need some remounts."

"The only horses I could find you are Texas mustangs, and I know the quartermaster doesn't buy them."

Woolard stopped and looked hard at him. "How far away and how long to get them here?"

"Telegraph John Doyle in Fort Worth. He can get them if anyone can, and have him ship them on the Southern Pacific. They should arrive at Deming in a week or ten days."

"Is this Doyle honest?"

"He'll do what he says he'll do."

Woolard stopped and squeezed his chin. "What will they cost?"

"Forty bucks a head, freight and all."

"At Clanton's sale, those sold for over two hundred dollars a head."

"You can get five for one at that price."

"Crook won't like them, but they'll damn sure beat walking."

"They're going to be tough as shoe leather."

"Nothing else I can do. See you—and, Slocum, be careful. I'll need you."

"I will be, Colonel. Careful as I can be. Chako and I will be at the border tomorrow night."

"Good—and thanks for this Doyle's name. I'm ordering them."

Back at the springs, Slocum met Chako. "We need to go back and learn all we can about Diaz and the broncos."

Chako nodded. "We ride at first light?"

"Yes, and try not to make Chewy mad."

With a bob of his head, the Apache sprung on his horse. "See you before daylight."

Slocum dropped his gaze to the sandy wash at his feet and shook his head in defeat. "Your neck." And his scout was gone.

"Time to ride," Chako said, squatted near him in the predawn gray light the next morning.

Slocum sat up in his bedroll and yawned. "Damn short night, huh?"

In the shadowy light he could see the grin on the scout's face. "You got to sleep."

Slocum cocked a questioning eyebrow at him. "Well, I sure hope you don't fall out of the saddle today."

"I have the horses."

"Good. Got any hot coffee?"

"She has." Chako gave head toward the small fire and the small figure squatted close by tending the coffeepot and some pans.

"What's her name?" Slocum asked, pulling on his boots after emptying them of any vermin that might have crawled into them overnight.

"Not important—she will have coffee ready in a little while."

"That's a damn strange name for an Apache—Not Important." He busied himself rolling up his blankets and then shaking out the canvas ground cloth.

Chako never smiled or frowned. He also, Slocum figured, had no intention of telling him her name. Soon she brought him coffee in a tin cup, and she didn't look familiar. She wasn't Chewy's wife anyhow. In a short while she delivered some flour tortillas wrapped around some beans and meat, with plenty of hot peppers, on a tray. Then she squatted close to them and waited until Chako told her in Apache that they were good. She nodded and smiled.

"Gawdamn good?" She looked at Slocum.

"*Sí, muy bueno.*"

She giggled, and then after a string of words for him that Slocum could not translate, she rose and left them. In a run, she hurried off out of sight in the shadowy brush, as if late for another mission.

"She have to cook another breakfast?" Slocum asked.

Chako barely bobbed his head, and held up his burrito to speak with his mouth full. "She's a better cook than Chewy's woman."

Oh, well—they were off to Mexico. Or they would be in a few minutes, he and his no-sleep scout, headed for the line. He'd missed another chance to stop off and see Mary Harbor—that left a taste in his mouth the hot peppers couldn't erase. So many wonderful women in this land and he was all the time thinking about a willowy schoolmarm—some memories just were more indelible.

Three days later, they were in Arido, enjoying some mescal in a cantina. An attractive young olive-skinned woman was dancing to fast guitar music, and the assembled vaqueros and riffraff were clapping to encourage her. Slocum could tell she was enjoying the attention, when a man slid into the booth.

"They tell me you are looking for Diaz."

Slocum turned and said to him, "Not me, amigo."

"I do not work for him. But I can tell you where he is at."

"At his hacienda?"

"No, he's gone to rob a stage across the border."

"When?"

"Tomorrow."

"Where?"

"Between the border and Benson."

Slocum moved his chair around to look the man in the eye. The room was fogged in smoke, and he wanted to look close at this man and test him. "Why tell me?"

"I figure you want him."

"And if I do?"

"Then you will pay me a reward."

"Telling on Diaz can get you killed."

"Many things in Mexico can get you killed. What is my reward?"

"Ten pesos now. Ten when I learn the truth."

The man smiled. "You are a tough man to help."

"If this is a trap and I survive, then you will get a ten-cent bullet in your gut. You savvy that?" Slocum counted the money out on the table.

"*Sí*. He will rob the stage, mañana."

"What's your name?"

"Rapheal Tellas."

"All right, Señor Tellas, I will see you in a few days with ten more pesos."

"Good." He stood up. "I am going to spend one of them on a *puta* now." He grinned big and headed for the bar. The teenage girl looked up at him when he touched her on the shoulder, and Slocum could read her lips: "No *dinero*, no pussy." But when he showed her a peso, she hugged him like a long lost lover and they hurried out the back door.

"What do you think?" Slocum asked his stone-faced scout.

"He could be a liar. He could be a Diaz man. And he could just want pussy." He shrugged and tossed down some mescal.

They both chuckled.

"We better get our horses and saddle up. I'm going to wire Woolard and hope he can send some troops in time. Maybe get the message."

The music started again, and the men clapped for the dancer as she returned. The loud, hard strum struck a chord and she was off again. Slocum took a last look and smiled. Pretty enough girl—he wouldn't mind taking some dance lessons from her.

The message in a code was left in the local telegraph office and Slocum paid the man.

Colonel Woolard, Fort Bowie,

    Same general workers stage strike again. Tomorrow below Benson.

                                  Slocum

He felt certain that Woolard could read it and figure it out. But it had to get to him first on a very undependable service, which was what he wondered about as they cinched their horses and prepared to ride out.

"What can we do against so many?" his scout asked.

"Be damn careful."

"Damn careful," Chako said and reined his horse around. They left Arido in a long trot headed north and with a good twelve-hour ride ahead of them or more. Slocum worried about their horses. They'd pushed those coming out of Mexico the last time too hard and ended up afoot. With good mounts so short in supply, he had that on his mind all night under the stars as they hurried north across the flat greasewood-clad desert.

They crossed a small range of hills and Chako picked up tracks. They stopped under the starlight for him to examine them closer.

"How many of them?" Slocum clutched the saddle horn in his hand and rocked back and forth in the saddle to awaken himself.

"Maybe fifteen, twenty horses."

"Could some be pack animals?"

Chako nodded. "They might need some to carry it out, huh?"

"I am thinking that."

"Most of his men are outcasts, but there will be some that could be tough fighters. Some Yaquis."

"Routing them is what we need to do. Let's go." Slocum reached in the saddlebags and began to arm a couple of sticks of blasting power with caps and cords as they rode through the silent, deep canyon and then up the steep trail over the pass. A fresh, cool wind swept his face. He had six sticks ready as they both searched the pearl-lighted desert beneath them.

"There, see the fire." Chako pointed out the red dot across the flats.

Slocum nodded. "Okay, lets give them a wake-up, then we can fall back to here and keep them from using this shortcut to the border. Maybe by then there will be troops."

"What if they don't come—the soldiers?"

"We'll be on our own."

Chako laughed. "Hope there ain't many Yaquis with them."

"You sound like those Chiricahuas. We use rocks on the Mexicans, and bullets we save for the American soldiers."

"What do we do?"

"You take some blasting sticks and scatter their horses. I'll toss some in their camp." He booted the bay in close and handed him the sticks.

Chako nodded and headed his pony to the west. "Have big bang, huh?"

"I hope so."

In the predawn, Slocum rode through the stirrup-high greasewood. He doubted Diaz had any sentries out, but he kept an eye out for any sign of one. Chako had dropped off into a wash to make his approach on the horse herd from that side. Slocum hoped his plan worked, and unless some straggler was up taking a piss and noticed him, he should reach throwing range. Obviously some camp followers were up preparing food; those women were at the fire and occupied, he hoped, enough not to notice his horse's soft snorts.

At last he could see the scattered bedrolls. He hoped Chako was in place. He used a thumbnail to strike a match from his vest and touched off the primer cord that spewed sparks as it consumed paper rope. He drew back and tossed the stick, then set heels to the bay and charged on into camp. The explosion behind them sent the gelding's tail clamped to his ass in a new burst of speed. Slocum lit and pitched aside another stick. Explosions were going off on the other side as well. He could hear the excited horses scream in panic and the thunder of hooves. Diaz's army would be afoot. He aimed the last lighted stick at the tent setup and wondered if it was the *general's* quarters. Then he reined the bay aside two screaming women running for cover, only inches from being run over by his horse. Pushing the bay hard, he headed for the pass in the dark outline of the low, jagged peaks.

Sounds of the angry soldiers and others shouting profanities behind him, he smiled catching up with Chako and the well-organized herd of animals headed for the hills. Who gave a damn what they were mad over—walking back across the desert would teach them respect and also brew more talk of revenge. *Diaz*, he thought, *your days as the great leader may be*

numbered—if the troops arrive before you can cross the border.
Slocum pushed the bay to the left to direct the herd more right.

Twice he'd taken Diaz's horses; this might be the one where
the *general* exerted his full-force fury against him. Like those
men he sent to the Madres foothills to get revenge for him over
the first horse theft. *Come on, Diaz, I'll be waiting in the pass.*

Slocum closed his eyes—till the military arrives. His greatest
fear lay in some Mexican telegraph failure—*Damn Woolard,
you better come help us fight those hornets we've stirred up.*

Two hours later, the sun still on a long slant, Slocum scanned
the desert with his brass telescope. The unorganized bandits were
ambling across. He could see one man with gold epaulets on his
shoulder, bareheaded, waving the rest forward with his arm.

Rifles loaded and ammo beside them, he and Chako waited
on their bellies for the bandits to get within rifle range. The
wind had picked up from the south and dried their sweat-soaked
shirts. Blasting sticks were set downhill as the last defense of
their position.

Slocum handed the scope to his scout and then wiped under
the leather headband of his hat with his kerchief.

"See him?"

"Ah, the *general* is coming." Chako laughed. "I can hear him
cursing already."

"You would too if you'd lost two herds of horses to the same
guys."

"You think he thinks Clanton stole them?"

Slocum sucked on his lower lip and shook his head. "No
telling. See any dust of an outfit coming to help us?"

"No."

"That's what I thought." He shook his head—no army in sight.

In half an hour, Diaz and his bandits reached the bottom of
the pass. Slocum nodded to his man. "Time to scatter them."

On his knees, Slocum sent hot lead at the ragtag army. The
shots from Chako's rifle took down a number of the men in
sight too. The rest scrambled for cover.

"Damn you bastards!" Diaz swore and shook his fist at them.
"I'll get you if it's the last thing I do."

"I had a Sharps .50-caliber, you wouldn't make that threat

again," Slocum said, with his eye slitted and the iron sight centered on the man's chest.

"Look to the north," Chako said, pointing with his rifle. "Dust. The army is coming."

"Not one moment too soon—" Slocum ducked after a bullet ricocheted off a rock close by him. "Damn, they can shoot."

"They see the dust too. How we hold them?"

"Make them stay down. We'll take turns shooting at them."

Despite their efforts, Diaz's army began to disperse; some ran east, some west, and next thing the *general* was simply gone. He'd crawled off under the belly of his own army. Slocum couldn't see any sign of him, and the last holdouts were breaking and running for cover in the nearby wash. That would leave the wounded for the U.S. Army.

"How many horses in the canyon?" he asked Chako.

"Maybe twenty."

"Good. We'll send them back to Woolard. He's short some."

"What we going to do?"

"We're going to be waiting for Diaz to return to his hacienda."

"Then what?"

"We wrap him in a blanket and pack him back up here."

Chako chuckled. "He will really be mad then."

"Gather those horses. I'm going down and meet that West Pointer that's bringing those troops."

Chako was gone, and Slocum went for his bay. Mounted, he headed off the mountain's steep side as the troopers drew closer. Two Apache scouts reined up and looked at the scattered wounded and dead.

"Big damn war here," Chewy said and grinned at him.

Slocum nodded. "You got here too late for the fun. Who's in charge?"

"Fairweather, lieutenant."

"I'll go meet him. Chako's got some horses we stole from them. He's bringing them up. Maybe some more of this bunch left, but they split here."

"Slocum, you having all the fun?" the bushy-mustached Sergeant Vonders asked, reining up his troop.

"No, they all ran off, both east and west. Diaz is with them."

"Divide up and go in pairs." Vonders directed the men to split up and look for the rest. "And don't wait. If they offer any resistance, shoot them."

"Lieutenant, my scout's bringing the horses we took from them. Some should make remounts."

The shavetail nodded in approval and checked his sweaty, head-bobbing horse. "Colonel Woolard said if you were still alive to give you his regards."

"Tell him Diaz got away, but we did stop the stage robbery."

"I am sure of that," Fairweather said, "and the mounts you confiscated will make him smile."

"There are five wounded and three dead here, sir," Vonders reported.

"Good job. We'll secure an ambulance and take them back to Bowie." Fairweather turned back to Slocum. "And you, sir?"

"We have business in Mexico. Any word on the gunrunners?"

The lieutenant nodded. "The word we received said they had the guns and were headed to meet the broncos."

"Where did they cross the border?"

"Scouts think they went through the San Pedro River Valley. Some Mormons at Saint David must have helped them. Reports are they had some stout mules."

"They wanted to go through there to make the distance to the old man's shorter." Slocum looked at the sinking sun. When they left that goat herder shack in the Oracle country north of the Catalinas, they really had more purpose than simply moving. They were headed for the mules, probably financing, and from there to old man Clanton's for the rifles.

"What are you thinking?" Fairweather asked.

"Old man Clanton's is not far from here. Loan me your scouts. Maybe I can stop them."

"Fine, but we aren't supposed—"

"You can just call us mercenaries."

Fairweather smiled and nodded. "Sergeant Vonders, find Chewy and Bee Tree. They're going with Slocum and try to head off the gunrunners."

"Yes, sir!" Vonders bounded onto his mount.

At the sounds of horses above them. Slocum looked up to

see that the scouts were bringing the Diaz horses off the pass. It would be dark in another half hour. Clanton's was three hours away. Maybe sometime he'd find some sleep for his gritty eyes.

"Thanks. Give Woolard my regards," he said to the officer.

"I will, Slocum. I will."

A quarter moon had risen by the time Slocum held their horses in a dry wash over a quarter mile from the big house, while his three scouts checked out the Clanton place. He'd considered napping, but knew he might never wake up once he shut his eyes. Close to thirty-six hours of being awake had him more numb than he needed to be in case of their discovery.

Chako returned like a soft night wind. He handed Slocum a warm burrito.

"Where did you get it?"

"Stole it. They're coming. No pack mules in the pens."

He wanted to know how his man had stolen his supper. But instead he nodded and took a bite. Not bad, and it was fresh too.

"No mules," Chewy said, joining them.

"Any been here?"

"No sign. Maybe one or two that belong here."

"Okay, Fairweather said they had mules and came through Saint David with the help of some Mormons. Have they not gotten here?"

"We can spread out and find them if they're coming."

"Any of you see any case of guns and ammo?"

Bee Tree shook his head. "Plenty stuff there."

"He has lots he has stolen," Chako said. "There are wagons full of it."

"No time to go back and look. I'd never thought, but he probably stole those rifles in the first place, like he rustles cattle to sell to the army."

The scouts laughed and bobbed their heads, amused at his discovery.

"We better split up and look for Slade and Thorpe. We can steal their mules or whatever to stop them—do it. Where should we meet?"

"There is a good spring and jacal near the Grande Arroyo," Chako said, and everyone nodded.

Slocum knew the place. "We'll meet there tonight. Take a siesta when you get clear of here. Then look for those two, but be careful—they'll sure shoot you on sight."

"We need to steal the mules or kill them, right?" Chako asked.

"Yes, if you can't steal them—shoot them." Slocum shook his head at the notion. Be a big waste, but he had to stop those two at any price.

Once clear of Clanton's, Slocum found he had a hard time staying awake in the saddle and sought a dry wash off the beaten path. His horse hobbled and tied so he couldn't run off, he undid his bedroll and spread it in the lacy shade of a mesquite. With plans to only sleep a few hours in the morning's coolness, he put his six-gun beside him and closed his eyes.

They were masked riders and he couldn't see their faces. Shots zinged past him and he could not get his Colt to fire. The hammer would not fall and he fought it as they drew closer and closer. Then he woke up in the sweaty brilliance of midday. Sitting up, his six-gun in his hand, he cocked the hammer then carefully released it—no problem. The bay snorted softly, close by obviously still asleep—tired as his owner. He mopped his wet face on his kerchief and tried to focus his dry eyes. Take a week of sleep to ever recover, he decided, and rose, sweeping up his blankets and canvas ground cloth. Better get moving. Maybe his Apaches had found them—he certainly hoped so.

He was a few hours from the jacal. Better head that way and be certain it was safe. Bedroll strapped in place, he undid the hobbles and tightened the girth. *Time to get on the move, ole hoss.* He took up the reins and swung into the saddle. On board, he headed down the wash listening and looking hard—the dream of his gun failing to fire haunting him.

On top again, he saw nothing but more bland greasewood flats and some saw-edged purple mountains in the south, dazzling in the heat waves. Setting the bay in a long trot, he headed for them and his destination. If only the Apaches could find the gunrunners . . .

Late afternoon he arrived. No scouts in sight, he approached it with care. No signs were evident in the dust that anyone had been there in recent times. He unsaddled the bay and let him roll, then hobbled him to let him gather what dry grass he might find. The shortage of feed for their animals would soon be the limiting factor in their staying out there. In the next twenty-four hours they needed to find them some.

He made a small fire and cooked some crushed-corn-and-brown-sugar gruel in a tin cup. It would give him some energy. Squatted on his heels, he watched the mixture plop and boil, making small splatters. When he felt it was cooked enough, he used his kerchief to set it off to cool. As the saliva filled his mouth thinking about eating the gruel, he daydreamed about good meals from the past and the lovely women who'd cooked them for him. Whew—this scouting could be drudgery. What was Mary Harbor doing?

"Don't move a muscle, hombre," the tough Mexican-sounding voice behind him ordered.

The person stepped inside and drew the six-gun out of his holster. Cold goose bumps popped out on the backsides of Slocum's arms despite the heat.

"Who in the hell're you?" Slocum asked in Spanish.

"His name is Pedro," a second voice said. "My name is Diaz. You must know me. Twice you have stolen my horses. You and some Apaches, huh?"

"You have the wrong man."

"No, you killed some good men of mine I sent after you too, huh?"

"Killed?" Slocum frowned at the man.

"The only way they would disappear off the face of the earth, huh?"

"Who were they?"

"Oh, you know so little, huh?"

"My name is Tom White—"

"Ah, but the Apaches call you Slocum, huh?"

"What Apaches?"

"One they call Bee Tree?"

How in the hell did he ever get his hands on the scout? Slocum felt his throat constricting. Less than a day ago they'd put Diaz and his army afoot and running for their lives. Since then Diaz'd obviously captured one of his scouts and tortured info out of him. Torturing Indians was considered a useless effort—Diaz must be the expert at it.

"Never heard of him. My name's Tom—"

The force of Diaz's boot slammed into his back and sent him sprawling facedown. For a long second he lay there in the dust to consider his alternatives and who might help him. Without an answer, he began to rise.

"Tie his hands behind his back," Diaz ordered. "We'll take him back. Those other scouts will follow and we'll roast all their balls over some red-hot coals."

"*Sí, mi general*. Get up." The burly Mexican, Pedro, jerked him by the arm to his feet. Then with a small rope he bound his wrists behind his back and shoved him down to sit on the ground.

Squatted on his heels, Diaz wiped a spoon on his leather pants to polish it. Then he ate the cup of gruel. "Not bad," he said waving the spoon about. "Maybe you would make a cook."

Slocum never answered. Answers only gave them reasons to get angrier. He'd save his strength for the hours, perhaps even days, of captivity ahead.

"You know you ruined my chances of getting the thousands in gold from that stage?"

No reply.

"Ah, you don't wish to talk to me?" Diaz beat the spoon in his palm.

No answer.

"You think the fucking U.S. Army can come down here and get me?"

"They get mad enough," Slocum said.

"It would mean war with Mexico!"

Slocum shrugged like that meant little to the army.

"Listen to me!" Diaz used his fist to raise Slocum's chin. "I will defeat them. Mexicans from all over would rush to my aid. Thousands would come help me slay your army. To fight you fucking gringos for invading their land again, you understand?"

"You don't really want war with the U.S. Army."

"Why not? They can't stop the bronco Apaches. I do not fear them."

"Your men did not stop and fight today."

Diaz looked at his dusty boot toes and nodded. "I did not have them ready for such a fight. A few more months they will be ready."

"Good."

"You say good, why?"

" 'Cause then we can send the buffalo soldiers."

Diaz frowned. "Why them?"

"They like to eat the ones they kill. We wouldn't have to feed them for several days after the battle. They can eat Mexicans and we'd save the U.S. Treasury some money."

"You ever hear of such a thing, Pedro?"

"No, *mi general,* I never hear of them doing that."

"Old African custom," Slocum said.

"Those sumbitches won't eat my soldiers. They will die where they stand!"

Slocum nodded and went on. "They usually boil them,'cause they say male Mexicans that age are tough to eat. Like old boar hogs, they smell real strong when they get the water hot."

"What in the hell do you talk about—cannibals? The U.S. Army has cannibals?"

Slocum nodded, matter of factly. "Hard to break old customs."

"Pedro, you find out about those black ones stationed at Huchuchua."

"Sí, mi general."

"Sorry you missed your meal." Diaz pushed off his knees to rise. "Now we ride to my command post. But you must walk. Saddle his horse, Pedro."

"Sí." And the man fled the jacal to obey.

Slocum wondered how he'd ever escape this self-made general and his man Pedro. His own time was like sand in an hourglass, sifting down fast. He needed a plan before his mind was obscured with torture and pain. There would be enough of that when they reached Diaz's place in the Conchos. Diaz would make an example of him—for show purposes with his own men. *See how weak the toughest gringos are?*

Damn . . .

12

The sun came up and Slocum rubbed his gritty eyes with his fists. His cell felt cool, and without a blanket the fallen temperature had soaked into him and he shivered. Diaz's army slept. Only women moved about the low cooking fires, stirring pots—wrapped in cotton blankets against the chill, their heads covered by scarfs, some on their knees making tortillas on top of iron grills and holding suckling babies to their breast. His teeth close to chattering, he heard a soft hiss at the barred window.

"Yes?" he whispered, moving aside and rubbing his arms briskly, hoping for some warmth to stir inside him.

"Here and be quiet." A woman handed him something wrapped in a tortilla through the bars.

"*Gracias*, what is your name?"

"Gloretta. You helped me once."

"I need out of here—"

"Hush. The guard he comes back. I must go."

"Think of a way," he said softly after her.

A bob of her head and she hurried away.

Gloretta, not a common name. Where had he helped her? His mind was blank, except he knew he had one amigo in the camp and perhaps more. His mind went through past times and places searching for the incident she spoke about. Maybe if he could remember, then he could weigh what her strengths would

95

be against Diaz. Time, the shortest thing for him, would be the only way he might learn it.

Mid-morning he was marched at the gunpoint of two guards to the front of the main building. He faced Diaz, who sat in a high-back chair under the palm frond porch. Many of his soldiers encircled them. They wore bandoliers over their chests, partly filled with cartridges, and carried single-shot trapdoor rifles and in the sashes around their waists, some old cap-and-ball pistols. They were not armed with up-to-date weapons.

"Ah, gringo, today we wish to know the plans of the U.S. Army to invade Sonora."

"I'm only a scout. How can I know such things?"

"This Colonel Woolard . . ." Diaz's eyes narrowed. "You are his personal man."

"I'm just a scout."

"Oh, you are more than that. General Crook comes this week. What will he do?"

"Shit and piss when he gets ready, I suppose."

His answer drew laughter. How did this bandit clear down in Mexico know that Crook was coming and when? Damn, the man's intelligence was impressive. Probably the blessed Mexican telegraph got the word to him. If he ever lived through this ordeal, he'd tell Woolard to close that gap.

"You are not listening to me. When do they plan to attack us?"

Slocum shook his head.

"I have many ways to make you talk, gringo. Today I am nice, but my patience is very thin." Diaz held his thumb and forefinger a small gap apart.

Slocum looked around. "You tell all them about you wanting them to fight the cannibals?" An audible sound of shock came from the onlookers.

"That's a lie!" Diaz shouted.

With a shrug of his shoulder, Slocum looked up at a buzzard circling expectantly. "All you know is they haven't ate you yet."

"There is no truth in that story."

"Ask the Apaches. No, you can't, can you? They ate them too."

"Take him to his cell, and a few more days on little food and water will change his tongue. My compadres, he is here to learn the land for an invasion by the U.S. Army. They know the forces of Mexico are thin and they think they can take it with little force. I, General Diaz, will not let them in.

"Who is with me?" Diaz's ranting came from over Slocum's shoulder as they marched him back. *El general* would need to pep them up after his stage robbery had failed and his forces were routed in the field by a handful of Apache scouts. For his part Slocum would have to let his cannibal story simmer and ferment in the soldiers' minds. One thing to fight a gringo, but a black cannibal would make them all think. These people were extra conscious of such things. What could be worse than to be eaten by a black soldier? He was almost laughing when they shoved him roughly inside his cell and relocked the padlock.

"Hey, bring me some food and water," he shouted after the two guards, who were hurrying back to hear the man's speech.

Then he heard a hiss and hurried to the window. She quenched his thirst by filling a small tin cup with water several times, passing it back and forth to him. Then she issued a handful of jerky. She took pains to look around, and with her head wrapped, he only saw glimpses of the side of her face. None brought any recall.

"Tonight be ready—I must go." And she left.

Be ready for what? Escape, he hoped, chewing on the hard jerky. Too hard. It would need to soak longer in his mouth before he chewed on it. But at least he had received some water and food. He must pester his guards some when they came back so they didn't suspect her generosity.

Gloretta—who could she be? Heavens, he didn't need to look a gift horse in the mouth. What was Mary Harbor doing? Teaching abc's to children on a slate board. He stretched out on the hard bunk, clasped his hands behind his head and did sit-ups. Had to occupy his time or he'd go crazy in this pissy, sour-smelling cubicle.

A commotion outside in the afternoon forced him to go to the window and try to see what all the cheering was about. Three of Diaz's soldiers with hard-stopping horses reined up at headquarters, and across the fourth pony was a body. He could hear them shouting—"Apache! Apache!"

At the distance he could not be certain who they had, but obviously the man was dead. The bald-faced sorrel horse that bore the body told him enough. Those sumbitches would pay—damn them. He ground his back molars on the tiny grit clinging to them. They'd pay and pay big.

Diaz was shouting—he always shouted—"Bring that gringo down here so he can see what we did to his scout. Bravo, Manuel and you, Cortez and Phillipe. You have killed the worst one."

"Come on," the guard ordered and directed him with his rifle muzzle to come out and march down the slope to the headquarters.

Step by step on the gravel ground filled Slocum with dread. All the Apache scouts were loyal, hardworking soldiers in his book—none deserved to be treated any other way but as fallen soldiers in death. Showing off the corpse like some outlaw's was against the bucks' religion and ways as well. But what did these ignorant Mexicans know about that? They'd burned Davy Crockett's remains at the Alamo—many more as well. Disrespect for the enemy dead was a sign of ignorance. He stopped and looked at the expired scout on the ground. A knife stabbed his heart, but he never flinched an eye.

"Your boys have killed a bronco. He's one of Caliche's men. Now you'll have the broncos to fight."

Many men checked one another, questioning his words and worrying about what that meant for them.

"You lie, gringo!" Diaz shouted.

"Why lie about a dead man?"

Diaz's arm pointed straight at the corpse. "I have no idea, but he is one of your scouts."

Slocum shook his head to dismiss it.

"Take him back to his cell," Diaz ordered and tried to take a kick at him with his knee-high polished riding boots. He missed, but his cursing and grumbling rage sounds followed Slocum back to his foul ovenlike den. Door padlocked behind him, he sat on the bed's edge and buried his face in his hands.

They'd killed Chako. Damn their souls. He'd damn sure miss that boy. So would lots of women on both sides of the blessed border—damn, Chako being dead was hard for him to accept. The knot behind his tongue felt like it would choke him. He clenched his jaw so hard his shoulders shuddered in anger. *Diaz—your command is over.*

Then, his eyes tight shut, he tried to forget the smiling handsome brown face, but that only brought back more memories of the eighteen-year-old, born on Cibaque Creek and raised by his uncle after smallpox took his parents at age five. Chako knew the Madres and the rest of northern Mexico like the back of his hand, going on raids as young as twelve, to hold horses and kill some Mexicans too on his first war party.

To have been killed by lowly Mexicans would have disappointed Chako. Somehow Slocum would have to even that score for him. It might change the boy's place in the hereafter in Apache tradition, and it was something he'd have to do for him. He shook his head to try and dismiss his sorrow. It wouldn't ever be the same with Chako gone. Maybe he needed to simply ride on when he—if he—ever escaped this loudmouth tyrant. No, he'd seek some revenge for his departed amigo.

May it rain shit on Diaz.

13

"Slocum!" He jerked from half-asleep. Sounds of the instruments and the fandango going on down at the headquarters carried on the night. Laughter and screams rang out. Then some shots cut the night as the celebration continued.

"Yes?" he said with caution beside the window.

"I have the key to the padlock, but I must return it. He is passed out."

"I'll move to the door." A thousand questions flooded his brain. A horse? A gun? How far could he get? If they'd managed to kill Chako, he'd need all his wits about him to ever out-maneuver them.

He slipped out the door, looking at all the lighted Chinese candles strung up for the celebration down at the headquarters. Then he turned to her as she relocked the door. Lock closed and a smile at him in the starlight, she pointed toward the west.

"There is a *caballo* there in the arroyo."

He swept her up and kissed her hard. When their mouths parted, she sighed. "You must hurry. But I never forget you." With a rue-filled headshake, she pushed him toward the horse.

With a tug at his hat brim, he blessed her and ran for his goal. With no gun to adjust on his right hip, he wanted to put lots of space between him and Diaz. While they celebrated was the time. *Muchas gracias*, Gloretta—he still did not recall her, even after kissing her sweet mouth. Where had their paths crossed? Going down the slope on his run-over boot heels, he spotted the saddled pony through the mesquite.

He tightened the girth, speaking softly to the mustang, and with the reins gathered, he stepped into the unfamiliar stirrup and took a seat in the Mexican saddle. Turning the horse to the north, he left in a long walk until over the next rise; then he put his mount into a hard trot.

Looking to the distant, sleeping mountains that meant the United States, he decided to call the horse Charro. He hit a set of wagon tracks and short-loped him. With a jaw-dislocating yawn, he stood in the stirrups and shouted at the stars. "Diaz, your days are short."

His eyes squirted water and he wiped them on his sleeve. Damn, he'd miss that boy.

With the sun rising in the east, he sent Charro up the steep canyon trail through the junipers. A figure holding a rifle stepped out from behind one of the large, bushy evergreens and blocked the trail.

"Chewy?" he shouted and the scout's nod told him enough.

He dismounted the hard-breathing bay and led him the rest of the way up the cow-faced steep pathway. "Did they get Bee Tree too?"

Chewy nodded.

"Son of a bitch. I thought we got them."

"Nothing I could do. They jumped us in camp. I got away." He dropped his head and shook it in defeat. "But there were too many."

"How come you were waiting here?" Slocum looked around the mountainside and saw no signs of anyone.

Chewy gave a head toss and Slocum followed him around a big juniper. Two naked Mexicans lay staked on the ground—spread eagle.

"Señor," one cried out with great tears. "Save us."

"These men kill Chako?" he asked Chewy.

The bob of his head was enough. "They were there."

"No! No! We are poor peons."

"You wish to ride back to Bowie with me?" Slocum asked Chewy, ignoring the pair on the ground.

"Yes. But first I must fix them. I went and bought this sorghum," Chewy said and began to drizzle it from the crock jug on the screaming one, making small strips on his chest, back and forth, then on his dusty, shriveled privates and legs. Ignoring the man's vehement protests, Chewy finished by striping the Mexican's shaking face with the black sugar liquid. Then without any emotion, the scout stepped over to similarly dress his partner in syrup.

"Señor," the second one asked. "Shoot us. The ants are too slow a way to die. Do the Christian thing."

"Chako was my amigo. May the ants be swift," Slocum said and put a boot toe in the stirrup. "I'm ready to leave."

"Go," Chewy said. "I will be there in a short while."

Slocum accepted the Apache's words, reined Charro around and headed up the towering mountain. He could hear the hysterical one's screams until he went over the next ridge. The thought of the red ants forming lines to secure the sweetness, then start on the flesh. It would be a slow way to die.

The turkey buzzards would find them. They'd light in treetops and grow braver by the hour, until they finally floated down and hopped around on the ground. The great black birds would dance around them until they wearied of the two screaming at them, then hop in close and pluck out their eyeballs. Magpies would pierce them with their sharp probes, time and time again, taking beaks full of flesh each time. The soldiers would die in darkness, slow and torturous like they had savored killing Chako. He booted the mustang to go faster uphill.

Chewy would squat for a long time there without any expression on his solemn face—to be sure they were punished for his fellow Apache's death.

The sun was dying in a bath of blood when Slocum finally dropped out of the saddle beside Birch Turner's corral.

The big man's bass chuckling carried on the quiet night. "That you, Slocum?"

"Yes."

"Where's your scout?"

Slocum shook his head, waiting for the sorrow cutting his

throat shut to pass. Then he managed to speak. "Diaz's men killed him."

"That sumbitch—"

"Who came?" she shouted from the house.

"Slocum. Cook some more; he looks starved to me."

"Alone?"

"Yeah, alone. He lost his good man."

"Oh, my—" Then she went back inside the house.

"You trying to stop a damn general with a few army scouts is serious business." Birch leaned his shoulder on the corral gatepost and rolled a cigarette.

Fumbling with the sweat-soaked latigos, Slocum nodded and unthreaded them. The girths undone, he swung saddle, pads and all off Charro's back. Loose at last inside the pen, the bay, with his feet set apart, shook all over in relief to escape the saddle, then rolled on his back in the dust.

Ready to light his smoke, Birch gave a head toss at the pony. "Guess he's the general's horse?"

"Long story," Slocum said. "I'll tell you all I know."

"I've got some whiskey at the house. You need a good stiff one, and you can take all night to tell me."

"Good," Slocum said and looked around. "My last scout's coming. He's having an ant banquet with two of Chako's killers."

"Oh," Birch said as if he understood the deal, and led the way.

After eating several heaping plates of her good food and having a few drinks with his stories thrown in, Slocum relaxed for the first time in days and found himself getting drowsy. Birch loaned him some blankets, and he went to a jacal nearby the house and to go to sleep. When he pulled the cover over his shoulder and rolled over to sleep, there was still no sign of Chewy.

Dawn, he found the Apache squatted beside his hipshot pony at the corral.

"She'll have some food ready for us," Slocum said, with a head toss toward the house. "You ready to ride to Bowie today?"

Chewy nodded.

"We should be there by dark."

"Good."

"Let's go eat," Slocum said and started for the house.

"Saw some tracks of mules."

He stopped. "Mules? Think it's the gunrunners?"

"*Sí.*"

"Where?"

"South of the Muleshoes."

"Yesterday?"

Chewy nodded.

Slocum would have to send the colonel word on the Diaz deal. They had to stop Slade and Thorpe from delivering those guns. They must be headed for the San Bernadino Springs or they'd have taken the trail down south into Mexico already.

Slocum drew in a deep breath. "We better go find them."

Chewy bobbed his head in Apache fashion. "Maybe they go to Clanton's?"

"They were supposed to do that, but it's been several days. Maybe they had to raise the money somewhere—who knows?"

"You two coming to eat?" Birch shouted at them from the doorway. "Its going to turn cold."

"We're on our way." Slocum nodded to his scout. "We better eat while we can."

Chewy grinned big. "Be long time, I figure, before we do it again."

They both chuckled and headed for the house. Might be a real long time.

Past noontime, they reached the San Bernadino Springs and watered their horses. A few Mexican families who worked for the Peralta family lived there in an adobe compound. The success of the Peraltas with their extensive land grant had led to disaster. The large spring was in the direct route of Apaches from the Chiricahuas-Dragoons Mountains en route to the Sierra Madres. So life and ranching on this vast spread had been tenuous, to say the least, for the Peraltas. They maintained some presence there with a small cattle herding crew, but as in all the rest of northern Chihuahua and Sonora, thousands of deserted *rancherias* marked the landscape, some intact even and the cattle and horses turned out to fend for themselves. Between old man Clanton and his "cowboys" plus the Diné, there wasn't much value in a life in any part of this region.

"Hello, *mi amigo.* Señor Slocum," the broad-faced one said, carrying a repeating Spencer rifle in his arms and greeting them at the compound's adobe-wall gate.

"Ah, Tomas," Slocum shouted, and threw his right leg over the horn to slide off the saddle. Hand extended, he clasped the man's tough, callused one. "We look for two men come through here with mules."

"Mules, huh? Tough hombres."

"Tough enough." Slocum waited for his reply.

"Ah, *sí,* they were here yesterday and went south."

"What did they say they carried?" Slocum asked, loosening his latigos.

Tomas shrugged. "Never said."

"They're taking guns to the broncos. We need to buy some food and sleep a few hours."

"So they can kill more of us." Tomas shook his head in disgust. "I'd known that, I'd never let them water here. Come, we will find you food and a place to sleep. Bring the horses."

Slocum looked around as the sunset bled on the tall cottonwoods and large tank of water. "*Gracias.* Come on, Chewy, we're going to eat."

The woman was short that hustled around making them fresh-flour saddle-blanket-sized tortillas between her palms. Then she draped them over her hot metal grill and smiled at them. "My name is Alma."

"Slocum and he's Chewy."

She nodded, on her knees busy tending to getting their food ready like a whirlwind. In a short while she had some meat and bean burritos all rolled up and on a tray for them. Next she poured them cups of wine.

"How was your day?" Slocum asked before taking a bite.

"Oh, grandchildren kept waking me up all night. So it has been a long day."

"You look too young to be a grandmama."

At his comment, she shook her head as if haughty. "You are some gringo."

"I am sure you must have had the first one very young."

Then gathering her skirts, she stood up and nodded. "You will sleep in my casa, no?"

"Ah, I'm pleased you asked me."

"*Sí*." She took a tray of her burritos with her to serve to someone. In a swish of the dress she hurried away.

Chewy looked around then grinned. "We go at dawn?"

"We better. I'll have her fix us some food and some to take."

The scout nodded. "I will bring the horses at dawn."

"Good," he said, seeing her return.

"Come, my cooking is over for now." Her arm wrapped familiarly around Slocum's waist, she directed him up the narrow dark street, drawing some stares from the lighted doorways.

"I have some hot water, if you would like to bathe," she said, once she had drawn the curtain and closed the front door's drape. With a few flickering candles lighting the small shrine, he noticed she had a table to work on, along with a few personal things and a pallet on the floor in the corner. She filled the basin with steaming water as he toed off his boots.

"Sounds fine."

"Where did Chewy go?"

"Where do Apaches sleep?"

With a visible shudder of her shoulders under her blouse, she looked up and shook her head. "I don't know."

"He'll be ready to ride at dawn."

"I will have you some food ready too," she said, swinging the skirt free of her tawny, shapely legs. A smile spread over his mouth at the sight of her naked. . . .

He awoke once in the night and then, satisfied there was not any threat, went back to sleep cuddled around her firm ass. In sleep's arms he savored the experience again and floated away.

With the coolness of the predawn creeping through his blankets, he realized she was no longer under his wing, and he sat up to dress. He recognized Charro's cough outside in the darkness. Chewy was there, ready to ride. Maybe they'd catch the gunrunners before sundown.

Be damn nice to have that settled.

14

To leave Alma was not easy, but after breakfast she sent them away with a poke full of food. Slocum paid her five pesos and she hugged him tight for it. They were off before the sun rose over in New Mexico, he and Chewy riding in a long trot southeastward across the shadowy greasewood-bunch grass flats that stretched for miles. His belly full, a fine piece of ass behind him along with a good night's sleep, Slocum felt rested enough to push on after the gunrunners.

"Where will they stop?" he asked his scout.

"Maybe Arido. Or at the Mormon settlement."

"Corrales," Slocum said, familiar with the polygamist colony at the base of the Madres. "I'd bet that pair goes there since they had some support among the ones in Saint Davis."

"Maybe," Chewy agreed and bent over in the growing light to look at the tracks. "We can follow them."

Slocum agreed, and they rode on as the sun rose and the heat did too.

Midday, Chewy took him to a small spring, where they drank and watered the horses. Only an Apache would have known about the small water source in the vast desert. No vegetative signs gave it away, not even much sign of wildlife using it. But it was sweet, and they refilled their canteens. Squatted and eating burritos, they let their mounts rest for a short while, before hitching up their girths and riding on.

Late afternoon they descended into the valley of the Mormon colony, spread along the small water source flowing out of the Madres which watered their fields of grain and alfalfa and orchards of citrus.

Slocum rode to the home of a woman he knew. The adobe-walled house had a thatched grass roof and a dirt porch that extended around the four sides. A black dog barked, and someone came to the doorway using her hand to shield the sunset's glare off the ash-colored ground.

"Slocum?" the woman in her early thirties asked, sounding uncertain. She swept the honey brown hair back from her face, then put her hands on her shapely hips to study him.

He reined up and nodded. "That's me. His name's Chewy. How you been, Leagh?"

"Fine. What brings you to Corrales?"

"Looking for two men who rode in here today. One's named Thorpe and the other is Slade. They have pack mules."

"Some men with a train came and saw the bishop earlier."

"They ride on?"

"Yes."

"How long ago?"

"Maybe a few hours ago. I saw the loaded pack mules hitched at his house when I went to get some supplies. The bishop was talking to them on his porch. Then when I came back they were gone. What about them?"

"They're greedy crooks taking rifles to the broncos in the Madres."

"You sure? The bishop would never—"

"I believe that some saints at Saint David gave them the money to make the deal."

"But Bishop Robinson would never help them if he knew their business. We all live here in fear of those broncos striking us."

"Maybe I better go ask him."

"First you must eat. When did you two eat last?"

"San Bernadino Springs," he lied to her.

"Goodness, I'll fix you two some food. Put your horses in the corral, there's water and hay for them in there."

He looked hard at her. "We won't ruin your reputation—I mean us stopping here?"

She laughed. "No, I am free. Clarence Wallace divorced me in Arizona. You couldn't be any worse in the eyes of the faithful." She wrinkled her nose to dismiss his concern and waved them to the washbasin on the porch.

"We will," he said. "After we water the horses."

"I do that," Chewy said and took the reins from him.

When the scout and the animals went around the building, she frowned at Slocum. "That's not the same one—"

"No." He shook his head warily. "Diaz killed Chako."

"I'm sorry."

"So am I, and when I finish this rifle business, I intend to even the score."

"Who are these two men running the guns?"

"Couple of jack Mormons. They're nothing but outlaws. Slade threatened to assault a young schoolmarm he was hauling in a buckboard for the stage line out of Lordsburg. She fought and threw him off the rig and he busted his head on a rock. Thought she'd killed him."

"She must have been strong."

Slocum shook his head. "Just scared. Only thing bad was she didn't kill him."

"You can do many things when you're upset."

"You sure can. Well, do you own this place now that you're divorced?"

"The church owns it, I think. Anyway this is a co-op and no one owns it. I can stay here."

He rubbed his whisker-bristled mouth. A cup of real coffee would go good, but there would be none in her house—the saints didn't believe in it. He admired the swing of her shapely derriere under the dress as she worked cracking eggs and frying meat.

"The bishop have another husband picked out for you?" he asked, knowing the customs of these people.

She turned and winked at him. "I think he believes I am incorrigible and doesn't want me to be a burden on any of his men here."

Bobbing his head in amusement, Slocum agreed with a grin. "Then he knows you."

"Oh, I have some who come after dark and knock on my door. I usually fire the shotgun over their heads the first time— Oh, come in," she said, looking up at Chewy standing at her door.

Slocum waved the Apache inside and turned back to her. "What happens the second time?"

"I aim lower."

"Hope you like ham and eggs." She busied herself dishing it out on willow china plates.

"We can eat about anything. And have."

She wrinkled her nose at him. "I don't doubt that."

After her meal, Slocum rode his horse down to the bishop's dwelling. Dan Robinson was rocking on his porch and reading a week-old newspaper. He was a full-faced man with no beard; the sweat eased from the creases, and he mopped his flush cheeks with a towel.

"Hot today," he said and nodded. "Have a chair. Your name is Slocum, right?"

"Yes, warm enough. I understand that Slade and Thorpe stopped by here."

Robinson cocked a brow at him. "And?"

"They had repeaters and ammo for the broncos on those mules."

His face turned hard. "No, they were carrying some machinery to a mine that a brother has up there."

"Bishop, they lied to you. They bought those guns and ammo from old man Clanton with money from some of your people at Saint David."

A scowl spread over his red face. "Who would do such a thing?"

"Someone who didn't care who lived or died and wanted to make a profit."

Robinson leaned back in the chair and turned when a tall woman came to the doorway drying her hands. "This man is not of the faith," she said coldly as if to discredit his words to her husband.

"No, I'm not, but I don't need to lie about this deal. Slade and

Thorpe are a pair of worthless no-accounts. Their wives and daughters all work as doves up at Fort Thomas. I'm certain forced to do so by their husbands. When your people here face those broncos well armed, then you can believe they sure ain't saints."

Wide-eyed, the woman gasped in shock at his words and her jaw slacked in pale-faced disbelief.

"I'm leaving—but I have warned both of you about them." Slocum stood up, breathing through his nose, and nodded at the bishop; then he strode to his horse. They could defend those two outlaws till hell froze over, but they better wake up.

Robinson never offered him a word; instead he turned and talked to his wife in a soft voice. Slocum gathered the reins and swung in the saddle. He halted Charro and looked back at the porch. "Oh, they're real nice folks."

"You shouldn't talk like that around a woman," Robinson said to him.

"Maybe you'd like to hear about it from a young school-marm Slade tried to assault two weeks ago."

"Shut your mouth." Robinson waved a finger at him.

"When they assault one of your wives—then you can be mad." Slocum booted Charro into a lope. He had no time for them. They almost deserved what they'd get out of this deal—it might be a raiding party too.

"Come on, Chewy, we're going after them."

"What did the bishop say?" She rushed out with her dress skirts held in her hands in the bloody red of the sunset.

"They were taking mining machinery to some mormon in the Madres."

"Oh, damn." She came over to his stirrups. "Kiss me before you ride off mad."

He bent over and their lips met. Then he lifted her off the ground to kiss her harder. At last, heady with the honey of her mouth, he looked her in the eye. "Damn, Leagh, I'm sorry, but we need to stop them."

"I understand." She crushed her lips together. "Don't forget me."

"How can I?" he said, feeling helpless as he set her down. His guts roiled at the thought of what he was leaving behind.

The sweetness of her lilac perfume filled his nose. Swallowing hard, he tossed his head at Chewy. "Find their tracks. We're going to stop them."

"Take care," she said, looking sadly after him and waving as they galloped out of the village, crossed the irrigation ditch bridge and headed into the foothills.

Darkness soon came, and Chewy said they were close to the pair. They found some water and grass under some cottonwoods and sycamores in the starlight. Enough forage for their tired horses, and they shut down, fed their mounts some whole corn in morrals while they feasted on tough, pepper jerky. Sure wasn't like Leagh's food. Horses hobbled, they rolled out blankets and crashed on the ground. Slocum was still angry over the outrageous attempt at a cover-up of the two's skullduggery—mining equipment, his ass.

A coyote or red wolf howled in the night. Slocum felt for his Colt; the smooth red cedar grips in his hand, he raised up and listened. Real enough. Apaches used the various calls from wild animals to signal one another. There it came again. That sounded like a red wolf all right; he settled back under the burst of stars and soon fell asleep. He dreamed about the school-marm, and as always before they could encroach on anything serious, she went off the tips of his fingers and ran away. Maybe that was the way it always would be. Damn . . .

In the coolness of the predawn, he and Chewy boiled some chicory coffee in a tin can. The beans had not been well roasted and the chicory was bitter—but they used it to wash down the rock-hard jerky. All of Alma's burritos eaten, Slocum dreaded what they'd have next—whatever that would be. He drew up the cinch and hoped they found the gunrunners before the sunset.

He and Chewy set out in a long trot as the spears of gold shone overhead, piercing the peaks above them. Sunup was only minutes away. But it was past noontime when Chewy pointed across the canyon and, struggling up the far slope, Slocum could see the mule train winding its way skyward.

"Now we get them."

"Yes," Slocum agreed and rocked in the saddle, with his hand grasping the big wooden horn. *Now we get them.*

15

The gunrunners were camped on a long mountain bench in the pines. Slocum could see the smoke from their campfire. Pretty obvious thing to do in a place where wild Apaches lurked—maybe they wanted the broncos to find them. Slocum shook his head and crawled back from the ledge.

"You see more than two men with those mules yesterday?" he asked Chewy as they straightened and went for their horses.

The scout shook his head. "Why?"

"Just wondered if they had any help or a guide. Finding the broncos is never easy."

Chewy gave him a solemn nod. "Maybe why they have the smoke."

"Could be. But we better keep an eye out for the broncos. I don't want some buck slipping up on us."

The scout agreed and bounded onto his mount. "We can ride closer."

A mountain jay scolded them from a perch in pines. Did it know anything? Slocum smiled—if he had any sense, he wouldn't be there without more help. Losing Chako and Bee Tree to the *general* was a big loss to him—besides, Chako had had a good sense of things at all times. Chewy wasn't lazy, but he was not the same sort of person. They pushed up the steep mountain.

Charro buckled under Slocum, and then the report of the rifle came to him. He dove toward the up hillside, shaking stir-

113

rups as he went off. The impact of his left shoulder striking the rock slide sent a hard shock of pain to his brain. Sliding downhill in the loose rocks and chert, he glanced in shock at the cliff edge coming fast at him. He stuck a boot out and caught it on a bush, stopping his descent and spinning him crossways on the strip of loose fill. He managed to catch a solid rock and pull himself onto the ledge.

Where was the shooter? His hand sought his six-gun—the holster was empty. Lost it in the rock scramble. The sharp rocks underneath gouged him; the downed, still horse lay on his side thirty feet above him, and his rifle was sticking out of the scabbard on the up side. No sign of Chewy and his horse. His scout must have sought cover. No sign of the shooter either—he glanced back at the dizzy heights and far below to the canyon floor. Too close for him.

Did he dare move for the rifle? He might be far enough under the brow to not be seen. Maybe the shooter thought he'd gone off the edge. Good if he did, but he doubted the man had moved anywhere. With his forefinger he shaved the sweat off his upper lip; the rough rock surface against his chest, he chewed on his suncracked lower lip, considering his options: lie still or move for the long gun and become a target. Where did he lose his pistol?

The ache in his left shoulder grew tougher. He flexed it and felt nothing broke. Probably just bruised the hell out of it landing on it—but it would hinder his using it much. He should have listened to that jay—he knew a *bruja* in Guaymos who would have reminded him that birds bring warnings. Unlike that witch, he didn't know which ones to take serious and which ones to ignore. He raised up some to try and ease the pain. His impatience grew by the seconds.

He could die there too. On his knees, he prepared to make a dash for the horse. With a quick glance off the cliff edge under him, he looked upon some gliding buzzards searching for breakfast. A long ways down there. He must cross the same fill he had slid down to get to the horse, or go above it. If it gave way under his soles, it could be Katy-bar-the-door for him. The next slide might be his last. In a crouch, he considered his chances. Cross the slide. To go above it would expose him too much if the shooter was still up there—besides it would take longer to get to the Winchester.

"Where did that damn buck go?" someone shouted.

"He got the hell out of here."

At the sound of the familiar voices, Slocum's heart stopped. They were still up there.

"You get Slocum?" Slade asked

"I think. He went sailing off the bluff."

"Better think hard that he did, 'cause that sumbitch will be hard to kill."

Thorpe laughed. "Not unless he's got fucking wings."

"I'm going up here a ways and try to find that gawdamn Apache. If we can get rid of them . . ." The rest of his words were inaudible.

Slocum began to slip across the crevice filled with the loose fill. His first step, the rocks crunched and began to slip downhill under his sole. His second step gave way under him, and down on his knees he scrambled with all his might, churning more loose stones and losing ground. At last he found sure footing and caught his short breath on the far side, staying low, but listening to the slide he'd caused to rumble off the edge.

Had Thorpe heard it? He'd need to be deaf not to have. Charro's still form lay forty feet above him. The Winchester's walnut stock stuck out of the scabbard and shone in the bright sun. On his belly, he began to slither over the dry ground, stiff grass, and rocks toward the source.

A bullet struck the ground to his right and sent a spray of sand into his eyes. The shot put him into action. He raised to his feet and, running low uphill, began to race for the rifle. His hands closed around the wooden stock and he jerked it free, then twisted to the left, hoping to use the dead horse's body for a shield. If he had chosen the right direction, he'd have some cover. At last, behind the horse and on his back, he forgot about the sharpness in his left shoulder, jacked a cartridge in the chamber and waited for another shot.

Three rapid-fire rounds plowed into the dead horse like slugs striking a watermelon. Slocum bolted up, feeling certain that Thorpe was above him and to his right. The iron sights struck on Thorpe's tweed vest, and Slocum squeezed off a shot. His bullet shattered the rifle magazine on the long gun the outlaw held in his hands and knocked Thorpe on his butt.

Cursing and out of sight, Thorpe ran for a horse, and Slocum knew he could never reach the top of the hill for another shot at him. Instead Slocum frantically began to search for his Colt. He spotted it in the chert and looked warily around before he ventured out for it. Rifle cocked and ready in his right hand, he moved sideways to retrieve it. Boots set apart, he managed to stay on his feet and changed hands with the long gun. He bent over and swept up his six-shooter.

A little dusty, but it looked fine. He jammed it in the holster and fought his way back to solid ground. Nothing he could do for the expired horse, but being afoot in the Madres was serious business. And he felt satisfied from the distant jackasses' braying that Thorpe and Slade had ridden off up into the mountains.

When he reached the tree line, he looked at Thorpe's shattered Winchester's receiver lying on the ground. Damn sure Thorpe's lucky day. Slocum's own rifle set down, he used the disabled one as a bat, and smashing it on the tree to bend the barrel, he rendered that disabled too. No need to leave a weapon around that might be recovered. He looked southward in the direction the gunrunners must have taken. His best bet might be to go north off the mountain, find a horse and possibly his scout.

He set out down the back trail. Uncertain of the way that Chewy had gone, he hurried, flexing his sore shoulder and carrying the rifle in his right hand. It would be many miles back off the Madres to any civilization. Finding water and something to eat might be a challenge. He looked across the vast country they'd traveled over—being afoot in a wilderness could be fatal. That consideration and his sore shoulder only made him move faster.

The dizzy heights towered over him, and the desert floor miles beneath him yawned like the mouth of a large monster. With no clouds in the azure sky, the mid-morning sun glared on his hatless head of too long hair. He'd regret not having any head cover before it was over.

Then in the corner of his eye, he spotted some movement. It was a roan horse and a hatless rider making his way down the opposite side of he mountain. An Apache who'd no doubt spotted him or heard the shots. His heart pounded in his throat. How many bucks were there? Even at the distance this one was from him, he'd close as the day went on. Rather than try to hide, Slocum began to jog.

One Injun—there were more. His lungs began to cry for air. The soreness spread down the left side of his body. The pines began to change into juniper—piñon in the lower elevation, which could give him more cover, but he'd choose the place he'd meet them if he could. Distance between them—that's what he sought, and his soles scrambled over the gritty trail cut in the softer ground by years of wear from travel.

He stopped and looked off an overview. Nothing moved in the dazzling heat waves of the desert spread out under him. Maybe down there in the cottonwood tops he could see, there would be some water. Something he'd need in the next hours to replenish the sweat soaking his shirt and what he wiped off his face on his sleeve before resuming his way down. Where had Chewy gone? No sign of him since the shooting. He didn't believe the scout had abandoned him, only got out of harm's way and gone the opposite direction that he did.

At the edge, he could see their dust far beneath him like scrambling ants on the far wall of the canyon. Three Apaches pushing their mounts off the hill to get after him. He'd better hurry. Jogging down the steep zigzag trail wasn't all that easy, but he made some good strides. Lower down, he planned to leave the path and use the cover of the junipers. One against three weren't easy odds; those bucks knew how to fight, but he had to outwit and outshoot them. A good Sharps buffalo gun would be handy. He could pick them off at a distance—but none of them were lying around.

He reached the lower elevations and started to the right of the trail. Breathing hard, he dodged through the brushy junipers, seeking some ideal place to defend himself. None appeared. He slid on his heels down the next slope and landed on his butt for the last twenty feet.

Up and running again, he turned back expecting to see the black-striped face of a buck on his heels, but he saw nothing.

Another steep hillside and he hurried down it, this time keeping his balance and landing on the flat below standing up.

A sharp scream and he saw the buck riding low on a blue roan, bearing down on him. In his right hand he had a brass case repeater and in his hard-set eyes the intention of murder as he bore down on Slocum.

He dropped to his knees and took aim—squeezed the trigger. His barrel burst forth with lead and gunsmoke that swept back to burn his eyes. The roan horse cartwheeled end over end and mashed its rider under his tumble. Shaken, the pony drew slowly to his feet, and Slocum rose with care, not taking his gaze off the downed one. Where were the others? The crushed Apache did not move—he must be either dead or unconscious from the fall.

In a low run, Slocum ran over to get the buck's rifle. The carbine swept up in his left hand, he headed in a long lope for the cover of a juniper and crouched there to get a handle on the others. Slocum's breath came short and pained as he tried to regain it. The sweat dripping, he studied a hipshot roan fifty feet away. The pony might be his ticket out. Two more bucks had been with this one—somewhere out there.

He didn't dare make a move until he learned where they were. A fly or two buzzed by him and some quail whistled nearby. No Apaches. Some doves cooed and then flapped their wings as they left a nearby juniper.

Was that a sign? Through the sights on his rifle, he studied the thick evergreen boughs. Make a move and he'd nail him. He dried his left hand on his pants. The bitter smell of spent gunpowder in his nostrils, he listened hard.

Then a buck burst out of the boughs that Slocum was staring hard at, brandishing a cap-and-ball pistol aimed at him. He looked down the sights and fired. Behind him a war cry cut the air as another Apache bore down on him with a tomahawk. Slocum was bringing the rifle around. Another shot rang out, and the racing Indian jerked his head up and broke his stride as a second bullet struck him in the back.

On his feet, Slocum was ready to bust him with his own rifle, when the buck wilted into a pile before him. Riding down the bench through the junipers with a smoking pistol in his fist was his scout Chewy.

Slocum dropped his chin and shook his head—too damn close.

16

The roan acted spooky, and riding him bareback with a rifle in his right hand made the job of staying on even harder. Slocum kept his eyes on the brush of the slopes, expecting another ambush. Chewy rode ahead of him a few yards, and the Apache did plenty of head twisting too. Hours later, they found some potholes to drink from and water their horses. Little doubt in Slocum's mind, the gunrunners had made their sale by this time and his efforts to stop them had gone up in vapors. He smoked a roll-your-own, inhaled it deep and let the nicotine settle his anxiety and disappointment. Slade and Thorpe weren't that tough or smart; they'd simply had some luck and a smoke screen—Diaz for one.

Maybe if Chako had lived? He took another pull on the cigarette and nodded to himself. Big loss for him losing that grinning Diné. Maybe it was time to move on, he'd been there too long. Chewy had covered his backside or he'd not have been there to listen to the night insects. Still—

"What will we do now?" The scout squatted before him.

"I've been asking myself that same thing. They've delivered those guns and we might as well head in." He shook his head in disgust. "Hasn't been the greatest deal."

"Three dead broncos."

"Yes, but two scouts lost too."

In the twilight, Chewy nodded and sat on his haunches with his elbows on his legs.

"Guess you want to go back to Bowie? Two of us can't do nothing about Caliche. The two of us . . ." He shook his head. "Thanks, anyway. You saved my bread today."

Chewy shook his head to dismiss him. "You'd done that for me."

"I'd hoped so. We'll ride back to Bowie. Nantan Lupan should be there ready to close this chapter."

"Crook comes back?" Chewy threw up his head and blinked at him.

Slocum nodded then ground out the rest of the cigarette. "He's set on rounding up all the broncos if the Mexicans will let him in to go after them."

"Good. Plenty grub and many laughs. I been with him."

"He's a good soldier. Tough as nails, but good. Let's push toward Bowie tomorrow. Nothing we can do about them two."

"What about Diaz?"

"You've got the same notion I have." Slocum dropped his chin and exhaled hard. "I'd like to see him in hell too—but . . . there ain't no way you and I can buck him."

"Maybe get some scouts and get him."

"You mean some Apaches, huh?"

Chewey nodded. "They would help get him."

"Man, I don't know, he's got lots of soldiers. And he isn't as big a fool as you'd imagine. Don't need to underestimate him."

"Ten good Apaches and some blasting sticks."

"All we need are nine more Apaches and a mule load of sticks." Slocum leaned back on his hands and laughed. "All we need . . ."

"Bet we can find them."

Slocum sat up straight and looked him in the eye. "You can find the Apaches. I can find the damn explosives."

Chewey tossed him one of his blankets. "You need this. I meet you in five days near his place. I have plenty Apaches—you have the sticks go bang-bang."

"Deal. Where're you going?" he asked, wondering what his man was up to.

"See you five days near the Conchos." Chewy was on his horse and leaving.

Slocum stood up and removed his hat to scratch his head. That was the fastest he'd ever seen that scout move—he was going find a handful of bucks and be back. Now where in the hell could he get the blasting sticks?

He decided to sleep a few hours. Oscar, Oscar Sherlock would let him have all the sticks, fuses and cord he wanted. That and a good mule and he'd be ready—day, day and a half to get up to Oscar's place at Naco and then he'd be headed back to the Conchos. In his blanket he looked at the silhouette of his hobbled roan. He'd for sure find a damn saddle there too. The insides of his legs were sore from clamping the thin roan to stay on. He only slept for a few, got up and rode off hours before the predawn. Maybe he'd find some food.

Half-starved, he rode into Naco and dropped off the roan on sea legs.

"Hey, who stole your saddle?" some whiskered smart ass asked, laughing and pointing Slocum out to his buddy on the boardwalk.

Slocum narrowed his eyes and he glared back. "You ever had a .44 stuck up your ass and got a hot lead enema?"

"Come on, Wake, that sumbitch is on the prowl." His smaller buddy tugged on his sleeve.

"Screw him, Matt. Any dumb ass that can't keep his own saddle don't scare me none."

"Then you ain't very smart, partner." Slocum adjusted his Colt on his hip. "Shame you ain't got your Sunday suit on 'cause they're going to bury you in them filthy clothes you've got on."

"Wake, damnit—he'll kill you!"

The big man shrugged off his concerned associate's grab at his arm to hold him. "Guns or knives?"

Slocum charged up in his face, and before the big man could draw back his fist, Slocum slammed him over the head with his gun barrel, knocked off his felt hat and drove him to his knees, then gave him a kick in the chest that sprawled him on his back, the muzzle of Slocum's six-gun pointed at his heart. "You ready to die?"

"No! No!"

"Then shut your damn mouth about my rig. I'm on a short fuse. That belonged to a bronco Apache who killed my horse and I killed him. My own saddle was under that dead horse and I had no way to get it out—plus I wasn't waiting around for the rest of his bunch. So now you know."

"I-I didn't mean nothing." The man held his filthy hands up to ward off Slocum.

"You damn sure did. You're nothing but a half-drunk bully. Next time you spout off at me, I'll shoot you first and tell God you died, you savvy?"

"Yes, yes."

He holstered the gun and went on inside the cantina. Still raging mad, he ordered a double whiskey and pounded his fist on the bar to let some of the anger ease out.

"Oh, hombre. You are plenty tough one." He glanced down at the short *puta* who was twisting her pointed finger in his side. More than half-Indian, she had a nice set of tits that she showed off in the low-cut blouse. Sweeping her full head of hair back from her face, she smiled up at him. "That fat slop is a bully and he likes to twist the arms of working girls and make them cry."

Slocum glanced at the door. No sign of them. He turned back. "Can you get me some good food?"

"Ah, *sí*. What do you want?"

"Lots of tender fire-braised beef, sweet peppers, frijoles, fresh-made flour tortillas—"

"Where do you want it?"

"You got a room?" He looked around.

"Not here. At my casa," she said and hugged him, driving her breasts into his side above his belt.

"Oh, you can eat and then we can dance—"

"What's your name?"

"Rey."

"Where's this casa?"

"I will show you."

"Bartender, give me—aw, two good bottles of whiskey. I have lots of trail dust to knock out."

"*Sí, señor.*"

He paid the man and she led him outside. Once on the board-walk, she ducked under the rail and undid the reins. "He can graze at my place."

Tired sumbitch wouldn't go nowhere if he turned him loose. "Good."

"You want a shave and a bath too."

"Unless you want to crawl in bed with a dusty grizzly bear."

"Oh, no *oso.*" She laughed with the reins over her shoulder as she walked in the street and led the tired roan. "We will have much fun, *mi amigo.* I know."

He bobbed his head. Most of all, he wanted some food—his backbone threatened to gnaw a hole in his navel.

17

His head hurt. Naked as Adam, the cool morning air on his skin, he reached down and touched his dick. It was sore too. How long had they been on this fandango? She sat up straight beside him on the pallet and swept the hair back from her face. Her small, pointed breasts shook while she fashioned her hair back with a ribbon.

"How long have I been here?"

"Three days."

She ran her hands down the insides of her shapely bare thighs and made a face.

"You sore too?" he asked.

She looked over at him and nodded with a sly grin. "We have did it more times than I count."

"Three days . . ." He added the day and a half. Five days and he hadn't done anything about the blasting sticks. "Sweet thing, I need to go find a horse, saddle and see a man."

She made a face and then sprawled on him. Her small hands cupped his cheeks and she kissed him, moving over to sit on his lap. "I would send that boy for more whiskey and we could . . ." She slid back, reached down and gently pulled on his dick. "And we could do it till I see more stars."

"If I don't get busy, the damn army may fire me."

"Oh," she said, moving up against him so her nipples were in his chest and her cheek was on his shoulder. "We could make more love."

He scratched his head. It felt nice to be clean. It felt nice to have this wild mink on his lap, her musk swirling up his nose— a mixture of lavender and female scents that fed his brain. A little coffee and food might clear his foggy brain—but. The rise of his growing erection under her made her leap up and kiss him.

"Ah, *mi grande*, he comes to life." What the hell was another hour?

Oscar Sherlock's warehouse sat on the U.S. side, which was only a dusty line in the imagination of what looked like a double-wide street and two custom shacks a block down the way in the middle of Naco. One had a tattered American flag over it, the other a sun-faded Mexican one. The businesses faced each other. Drunks staggered in the international tourist business from a cantina across to a saloon, to further pursue their leave of the world they lived in.

Sherlock, who imported and exported, was a short man behind glasses that his small red eyes peered from under a green visor. How in the hell a squeaky-voiced little man in his forties like Sherlock did all the business he did, Slocum didn't know, as he wrapped the reins on the hitch rail.

"Slocum. Slocum," Sherlock repeated, and blinked against the midday sun at his first sight of him standing at the base of his dock tying up his horse. "Why are you here?"

Slocum glanced around to be sure they were out of earshot. "A little business."

"Well, well, come in. I'm always glad to see you, and happier I don't need your services."

"Good. I've got a project I need to handle. I need three boxes of blasting sticks, fuses and cord on the credit."

Sherlock glanced back at the roan horse at the rack. "A saddle, a damn site better horse and what? One or two mules?"

"One."

"Well, you're lucky I have all that. I do. I do."

"I am not flush with money."

Sherlock threw his head back to see out from under his visor. "Did I mention money?"

"No, but money would be nice."

"Sit down." Sherlock indicated a chair before his cluttered desk. "I owe you more than I've ever paid you. Lots more."

Seated, Slocum flexed his shoulders and arms. "This bandit Diaz killed my scout and another good one."

"You need all that to repay him?" Sherlock chuckled and shook his head. "When do you need it?"

"Oh—tomorrow."

"I know you. Know you well. Early. You get up before the chickens."

"Something like that."

"Martin! Martin!" Sherlock called out in his high-pitched voice.

In seconds, a fresh-faced youth of perhaps twenty stuck his head inside the office. "Yes, sir."

"Meet my friend Slocum. Good friend. He ever needs anything, you give it to him if I'm not here."

"Good to meet you." Slocum rose and shook the young man's hand.

"Yes, Mr. Sherlock says you're the best man he ever hired for collections."

"Martin, he needs that bay Morgan horse, a decent saddle and a mule with a good *aparejo*. Three crates of blasting powder stick, fuses and lots of cord—throw in some food."

"When, sir?"

"Before daylight tomorrow—here."

"They'll be ready, Mr. Slocum."

"Slocum."

"Yes, sir."

"Mind you, Martin, he will be here before a chicken even peeps."

"I'll have them ready. Anything else, sir?"

"I'm taking him to my house for lunch."

"I'll have Miguel bring the buggy around in a few minutes, sir."

"You are—you're going to have lunch with me and Marie?" Sherlock blinked at him. "Wouldn't miss it."

The spanking buggy horse single-footed and made fast time. They soon drew up the lane to Sherlock's fine white-plastered two-story house. A man came out and took charge of the horse and rig. Brushing off the road dust, they went in the front door and Slocum stood in the two-story living room.

A light-haired woman appeared on the balcony and Sherlock announced, "My amigo Slocum is here to eat with us."

"At last I meet the famous man." She swooned and hurried down the staircase. Mrs. Sherlock was an attractive woman hardly out of her twenties, with a sugary voice.

"Your husband exaggerates."

She took both of his hands, and from arm's length she looked him over and smiled. "Gods up close still are gods. Business bring you here?"

"Yes, ma'am."

"Show him where to wash up," she said to her husband. "I'll go tell the kitchen help we have a famous person here to eat with us."

"Make too big a fuss and he won't leave," Sherlock teased and showed him to the wash area. "You made a fuss the other day beating that bully with your pistol."

"You hear about that?"

"Heard about . . . about the fuss you had when you got in town. I suspected that was you; then you disappeared." Sherlock dried his face and hands on a towel and examined his cheeks in the mirror on the wall.

"People like that need lessons. I had business."

Sherlock smiled. "I had wondered where you were since then."

"Found a place to rest up, get a bath, shave and a haircut, plus lots of sleep the last couple of days. I needed it too."

"Good enough."

"Between Diaz and two worthless gunrunners named Slade and Thorpe, I've been running back and forth as well as keeping an eye on the bronco Apaches." For the first time in days he thought about the schoolmarm, Mary. How was she making it?

Sherlock frowned at him. "Oh, Jed Slade?"

"Same shiftless border trash."

"What was he doing—" Sherlock cut off his words at the appearance of his lovely young wife sweeping out of the kitchen.

"Plenty of food and may we have some of the good wine?"

"Of course," Sherlock said and hugged her shoulders. "How have you been, my dear?"

"Good, I have been busy all morning with the cleaning girls. Arizona is as dusty as Texas. I will go get a few bottles."

"I have to be back to work—"

Her index finger pressed to his lips, she shook her head, then twisted away in an alluring fashion for her skirt-swishing exit, with a pause at the doorway to say to him, "You can take a longer lunch today and visit with your old friend."

Sherlock made a face at her disappearance. "Lovely lady—but she all the time makes me take long lunches."

"Not bad company. Where is she from?"

"El Paso. Her husband left her there at a hotel and went into Mexico. He was killed by bandits across the border. They took all his money. She was destitute. I was there on business and it worked out very well."

Slocum agreed. The widower had needed a wife. Marie looked and sounded like the perfect mate for him—good.

They had a leisurely lunch. Sherlock's food had taken on more of a border flavor than in the past and Slocum savored it.

"You've been working for Colonel Woolard?" she asked.

"Yes."

"It must be dangerous. The Apaches and all."

"At times. I really think it's the meddlers that cause half the trouble, running guns and whiskey to them."

"Where will you go next?"

"Oh, I have more work to do down there."

"My," she said as if impressed and appraising him. "Don't you miss having a home? A wife?"

"I'm not certain."

"Well, why not? You're well educated and all."

"I guess, war and all, I've never known what a house and wife would be like. So I can't hardly know what I've been missing."

They laughed and Sherlock patted his wife on the hand. "My dear, Slocum has the sugar foot."

"What's that?"

"It is an itchy-feeling disease anytime a female mentions settling down."

"Oh, dear—"

"It's not contagious, I assure you."

"I hope not."

Slocum left Sherlock after they rode back to the warehouse. He offered him the bay horse, but Slocum thanked him, jumped on the roan and rode him back to Rey's casa. She rushed out to hug him when he dismounted.

"You have any use for this Injun horse?" he asked.

"Me?"

"Who else would I ask?"

"Of course I would have him. But what will you ride?"

"I bought another today."

"Where is he?"

"I get him at daybreak. Then you can have the roan here."

"Oh, you are too kind to me." She hugged his hip as he undid the bridle and let the roan go graze.

"I have two new bottles of whiskey."

"And you are leaving me?" She folded her arms and pouted. He laughed. "Ah, but what a send-off party we will have."

"Yes!" she shouted and took the bottles from him. *"Grande! Grande!"*

Slocum woke up the next morning before dawn. She was squatted at the fireplace under a blanket to ward off the cool air. Reflections of the flames illuminated her face in red orange when she turned to look at him.

"Ah, you are still alive," she teased and turned a tortilla with her fingertips on the sheet-metal grill.

"Still alive. But barely." He strapped on his holster and went out to relieve his bladder. In his bare feet, he stood in the starlight outside her jacal and listened. A few doves cooed and somewhere a dog barked. Nothing sounded out of place as he let fly an arcing stream of relief into the darkness. Finished, he shook it, put it away and buttoned up. Be a long ride to the Conchos. He'd have plenty of time to devise a plan—needed somehow to get those good women who'd helped him out of harm's way too when hell broke loose.

They rode the roan double to the warehouse. Rifle butt on his right leg, he circled and came in from the north. In the starlight, he watched close for anything. Some feeling of apprehension had ridden in his subconscious, since he had awoke—saying, *Take care, you've been at this place long enough to draw the attention of your enemies.* Far short of the corrals and the dark outline of the warehouse, he halted the roan.

"You suspect trouble," she whispered.

"Can't take any chance." He drew his left leg up and slipped off the right side like an Indian pony expected. Then he handed her the reins and gave a head toss to the north. "Ride off slow."

"You see something?"

His right hand adjusted his holster and he tried the six-gun, then, satisfied, switched the Winchester back to his right hand. She had not moved.

"Get going."

"You expect trouble?"

He shoved the roan around and set her on her way.

"Be careful, my lover."

He nodded and began to run low for the corral. When he reached the far side, he listened to the snores of sleeping horses and mules, the soft shuffle of hooves in the powdery manure base and an occasional grunt or squeal.

Where was the Morgan and the mule? Easing his way around the large set of pens, he saw a light on in the office. Maybe the boy didn't expect him so early. Then he stopped— two men with sombreros and rifles stood on the back dock. Damn—he wished he had not sent her away with the horse. If he hadn't, he could have simply disappeared on the roan. He should have known his presence this long in Naco would have been noticed and his plans leaked out. Too damn busy having a Roman orgy with Rey's sweet ass and not thinking like a man who needed to survive. Crouched down on one knee, he considered what to do next. Who did these gun toters belong to?

A horse was coming—he frowned. Someone drunk was riding it. He could hear a woman singing some dirty ditty about a lady with titties. Both men ran to the edge of the platform to confront her.

"Hello, *mi amigos*," she shouted and waved at them.

"Hush," one said.

"Oh, you don't want some fine pussy."

"I bet fine pussy. Go away. We have no time for you."

Slocum used the distraction to move in. "Drop the guns."

For a moment, one of them considered doing something, but then he too dropped his rifle.

"Smart man," Slocum said, covering them and closing the gap.

"How many more are there?" she whispered.

"How many are inside?" he asked them, relieving them of their sidearms and knives.

No answer.

"Somebody better go to talking," he said in a low voice to the two. But before he could stop her, she was moving down the platform to look in the lighted window.

She hurried back on her toes. "Three and the boy who works for him. He's tied up."

"Get on the ground. Facedown," he said to them and nodded to her. "Keep my gun on them."

The two grumbled, but obeyed. He ran to the corral, snatched a couple of lead ropes and ran back to tie their hands behind their backs and one foot to that so they could not do anything.

"You need to ride out of here," he said.

She shook her head. "Do they have your horse saddled?"

"I'm not sure."

"I'll go check." And she rushed off to the corral. Before he finished binding the second one, she rushed back. "There is a saddled horse and packed mule in the pen."

"Good. You find a saddle and toss it on the roan. You'll have to come with me or they'll hurt you for helping me." He gagged both of them and then straightened.

She nodded. "What about the others?"

"I better eliminate them too."

"Be careful," she said and then ran to the corral for one of the saddles on the rack.

He nodded and stuck one of the men's revolvers in his belt

for a spare. "Bring out the horse and mule. Try to check the load. I'll be back." He left the rifle and vaulted onto the platform. He found a sliding door unlocked and slid it gently to the side. In minutes, he was in the dark warehouse that smelled of raw wool, sweet grain and dry goods. He made his way through the darkness, toward the light coming from under the door, with his Colt in his fist. The men in the room were talking in Spanish.

When he sprung the door open, he'd have to find his targets fast. Percussion from the first shot in the room would douse the lights. The darkness and the boiling, acrid gunsmoke would be enough to blind the occupants as well as deafen all of them. An ear to the thin wood, he heard one swear and demand, "When is he supposed to get here?"

"How should I know," the boy said.

Six-gun in each hand, Slocum used his foot to smash open the door. He saw where the boy was and fired at the shocked-looking bandit on the left. His right-hand gun raised and aimed at the one by the door—it spoke hot lead and the boiling smoke burned his eyes. The third hombre dove out the window and Slocum rushed to stop him. Two rapid shots of a rifle came from down the platform and sent him sprawling off the side.

"I've got the other two," he said to her from the broken-out window as she rushed up with the smoking Winchester. "Watch the broken glass. I better check on the boy."

"You all right?" he asked, untying him.

"I'm fine."

The boy was coughing from all the smoke, and once he was released they joined her on the dock.

"Who were these men?" Slocum asked him.

"They worked for the general. After I had the horse saddled and the mule loaded, they jumped me."

"Well, if they live, I also have two more tied up outside. Turn them over to the law."

"I'll do that. They'll get some hard time in Yuma."

"Good. I'll go get the horses," she said.

Slocum agreed, satisfied that the young man was fine. "Tell

Sherlock I'm sorry about the broken window and thanks for the animals and explosives."

"You found them?"

"Oh, yes. We'll be fine."

"Be careful, Mr. Slocum, obviously General Diaz knows who you are."

"Obviously," Slocum agreed. He had lots of tricky things to do ahead. Maybe he could end the *general's* reign. He hoped so.

18

There was no sign of his Apache scouts when he found the small spring in a side canyon, several miles from the rancheria. He watered the animals and then they withdrew to an abandoned place with a palm-frond ramada and corrals good enough to hold their animals. With little feed for their animals, it would be hard to stay there long. Chewy would find them easy enough—the time was when?

The food Sherlock's man sent in the packs with the explosives was mostly jerky, frijoles and some flour and lard Marie used to make tortillas. Rey was as adaptable as most of her country's women, and wherever they were they could gather enough fuel to build a slow, hot fire and cook what was necessary to survive. Besides she occupied him in the long wait—she really liked her void filled with his dick any way she could get it and as often as possible.

She was taking a siesta when he heard the horses approaching. Rifle in his hand, he ran over and shook her. "Company."

In a flash of her bare brown legs, she rolled over on the pallet, pulling down the hem of her dress to cover her shapely butt. The rifle cocked, he knelt beside her and wondered who was coming. A patrol or Chewy?

Soon the red headbands appeared and Chewy booted his horse forward in a lope to join them. Relieved, Slocum went to join them.

135

"I see you found many," he said to his scout.

Chewy nodded. "Six more come tonight."

"That should be enough."

"Plenty. Who is she?" He indicated the sleepy Rey stretching and yawning under the shade.

"Her name is Rey. She saved me from the *general's* men at Naco."

"Good."

"She's going in the village and get Gloretta and the good women to come out the morning we are to attack them."

Chewy nodded. "Be dangerous."

"She knows that. But she is fearless."

"How many men are there now?"

"I don't know," Slocum said. "I have stayed away until you made it back so I didn't spook them."

"Good. I will send some men over there to count them." He moved back among the dozen riders that had came with him, and soon two rode off to do his bidding. The others dismounted, left their ponies ground-tied and joined them at the ramada.

"You'll need to cook more frijoles," he said to her.

She looked at the palm fronds for help and laughed. "Whew, there are mucho hombres here."

"If you are going in tomorrow to find Gloretta, you need to ride in looking for your cousin. Lupe."

"This woman's name is Gloretta?"

"Yes, she got me out their jail and then relocked it so they'd not know what happened."

"I will find her," she said, squatting down and looking over the dust-frosted scouts in a circle around her. "I can see they are hungry." Then she laughed, and they did too in an echo.

"I'm taking a siesta," Slocum said. "Now I've got so much help to be on the lookout."

The crew nodded, but their attention was on the cook, and he knew a good patch of cooked frijoles might fill them until they found the next meal. He gave a wave to Chewy and went to catch a few winks.

In his sleep, Mary again appeared and then slipped off his fingertips. He woke and found the sun low in the west. First real rest he'd found in days. He sat up, rubbed his gritty eyes, and Chewy, seeing him awake, came over to drop close and talk.

"There are maybe thirty men in his camp."

"The general's there?"

"Yes."

"Then tomorrow Rey can ride in and look for her cousin."

Chewy agreed.

Slocum scowled, coughed up a hocker and spat it aside. "Could be a bad place, but she's tough and I'd like the woman who helped me escape to get out."

Chewy nodded in agreement. "We will watch for the women."

"Good."

"Yubie has the layout." Chewy waved him over. The rest crowded around to grunt and agree.

The young buck used a stick in the hard dirt to draw where the men slept that did not have women. Then he pointed out the thatched building where Diaz stayed and where he thought they kept the guns.

"Come over here," Slocum said to Rey. "The way to get out of there is get in this dry wash and go north." He looked at the others. "Watch for her and some women coming out here. Don't shoot them."

The nods went around the circle, and Slocum turned back to see the place where Chewy said they should go, pointing out to the various ones where they should be. Slocum knew many, like Red Dog, Paunchy, Yellow Paint, Two Deer, Big Bird, Pony Boy, Tiger Man, and the others that were not familiar to him— all listened to Chewy.

Then he went for a section of fuse and showed them eighteen inches, lit the end and tossed it on the ground. The string sparkled like a firecracker fuse, eating up the strand, and when it came to the end, he clapped his hands and shouted boom! They all nodded that they understood.

The rest of the day they opened each of the red waxed sticks, implanted fuse attached to an eighteen-inch cord in the black granules, then closed the end and wrapped two more sticks in a bundle around that one. Soon the boxes bristled with loaded sticks, and by sundown they had the job completed.

Slocum trailed after Rey as she rode for Diaz's camp. He watched her turn up the canyon and from his high spot saw her pass through his guards, who made smart comments that carried to him, about a new piece of ass had come to them. They'd think "piece of ass" when they were blown to kingdom come.

Slocum finally could not see anything from his perch and slipped back to his horse. But he could hear the music—good, they'd have another fandango. They'd all be asleep at dawn, when his scouts struck them. *Get ready, Diaz. We're coming with the sun.*

In the cool predawn, their ponies hobbled in a nearby draw, Slocum and his scouts spread like black ants over the creosote-smelling greasewood-clad hills. A grunt or two and the guards were victims of sharp blows that delivered them to unconsciousness or death—then silence save for the soft scuff of hard moccasin soles. They split up and went around the buildings. An unfortunate dog or two made only a yelp and his throat was cut. Slocum at last stood on the porch of Diaz's headquarters. Six-gun drawn when a coyote howled, he considered holding his hands over his ears for the forthcoming explosions.

As he ducked his head, the next twenty seconds ate up the various cords, and the first explosion was in the barracks. The second one exploded in the side jacal, in a huge blast of dust. The thatched roof flew up and then collapsed back down. More explosions all over racked the camp. Women screamed and men shouted and cursed, and shots were fired.

Then the main man burst out on the porch brandishing a silver pistol and trying to put on his coat. "What's happening?"

"Drop that gun and get your hands in the air," Slocum ordered.

"Like hell—" Diaz swung the barrel around, but the turn was too great and that's why Slocum's first shot struck him in the chest. He still fired his pistol, but the shot went wide of its mark. Slocum's second blast of hot lead staggered him. Diaz's next round plowed into the ground beside his foot adding a cloud of dirt to the boiling gunsmoke. His knees collapsed and he pitched forward.

Slocum looked around, his .44 ready and the smoking muzzle

held high. The fight was gone from the soldiers as the sun began to spear red orange lights over the hills and onto the camp.

"You gringo bastard . . . I should . . . have killed you." Diaz strained to speak.

"Should have," Slocum agreed, kicking his silver six-gun away. "You should have stayed in Mexico. Gringos don't like robbers."

"But . . . your army has no authority . . . here."

"I see no army—only the Apache."

"Apache—" Diaz's words caught. "You . . . sumbitch . . ."

Slocum reached down and closed his eyes. "Sleep, *General.*"

Pony Boy came by the porch on a horse. "Gawdamn good whiskey!" He held up a crock of rum to offer Slocum a drink.

Holstering his gun, he stepped over and took a slug. Then held up the jug. "Good." And handed it back.

Pony Boy's eyes gleamed with excitement as he waved his treasure. "Have gawdamn good drunk. Fuck all the women! EEHA!" He rode off screaming like a coyote with hot pepper poured on his ass.

Slocum headed for the wash and saw some women coming out of the depression. Gloretta and Rey were among the five. He stopped them in the road.

"Them Apache bucks are wound up. They kinda plan to have a big party."

Gloretta look at the others. They shrugged as if it made no matter and searched one another.

"They won't kill us, will they?" one of them asked.

"No, but they might rape you."

"Oh hell, is that all," one said and the four headed for camp. Gloretta held back.

"Slocum. Thanks for sending her," she said. "We're sure even now."

Then she rushed to catch the others.

He shook his head and then grinned at Rey. "I owe you."

"Let's go raise hell with them then," she said and caught his arm.

He looked back and saw nothing out of place in the desert that stretched north. "Hell, yes."

19

The next day the scouts took the horses away from the remaining soldiers that guarded the herd in the tules. So with the scouts' new horses loaded with treasures and the village women mounted to go their own ways, they parted from the scouts. Diaz's men that were still alive found themselves left barefooted to make their own way out of this place.

The last thing Chewy's command did was blow up the headquarters full of ordnance that the Apaches had no need for, and watch from afar as the thatched roof blew sky high and spooked all their horses.

"Where will you go?" Slocum asked Rey as they headed north across the greasewood sea.

"Oh, back to Naco. I have friends and customers." She shrugged and reset the sombrero on her head. "Who would ever believe I was at the demise of the *General* Diaz?"

"There will be a replacement for him in weeks, I'm sure."

"Yes, in a week or less." She chuckled. "What will you do?"

"Go back to Bowie and collect my pay, if they have any money."

She rode in close and leaned her cheek on his arm. "I won't forget you, and you ever need any help again, remember Rey in Naco."

"I will."

"No wife, no hacienda?"

He shook his head. "A saddle for a pillow and sky for a roof."

"Then when you ride through, share my bed and roof."

He nodded that he heard her and looked at the fuzzy, distant purple mountains. He'd think long about the short Mexican woman and her strength—enough to shoot down a killer and go into an armed camp and save other women.

They parted in the night with a kiss and an embrace. He rode on with the scouts, who acted anxious to get back in the U.S. with their treasures of war. Why they felt any safer across the line he had no idea, but rode along. Mexico had no forces in the field that would intercept them this far north—but they passed on like silent ghosts into the Muleshoes and over the divide so they were heading up the Sulphur Springs Valley when the sun climbed over the Chiricahuas.

They reached Fort Bowie by mid-afternoon and red-faced First Sergeant Troy McCabe was stalking the scout camp. "Where in hell've you been and where did you get all this crap?"

Slocum rode into the middle of the shouting. "Sarge, they've been on a special tour for the colonel."

"Colonel, my ass, Slocum. General Crook's ready to hit the trail for Mexico and ain't a scout in camp when I needed 'em."

"Let's just say—General Diaz ain't making another raid over the border."

Hands on his hips, the big man scowled up at Slocum. "You and these gawdamn scouts took that bandit and his bunch out?"

"That ain't for newspapers. But Diaz is in the fires of hell."

"His gang too?"

"Yes."

"Shit fire, that's different. You scouts get ready. The old man is itching to get going come first light."

"We be ready," Chewy said and rode off for his wickiup, leading six laden horses.

"Where's Chako? Who else?" The noncom frowned and swiveled around as the others scattered in the junipers.

"Bee Tree and Chako. They ain't coming back."

"Aw, hell. You going up to see the old man?"

"I better."

"Damn right you better."

His report to Woolard took over an hour. He finished with a request for his pay and release.

"I can imagine you're worn out. But I wish you'd reconsider staying on awhile longer. Crook may end this damn war once and for all," Woolard said.

"Good. Save some lives. I'd like to request my pay anyway."

"We can do that in the morning. Maybe you'll reconsider. Getting that damn bandit Diaz down there where we could never have gone without an incident is a miracle."

"No, those scouts did it to even the score."

"I'm sorry about Chako. You counted on that boy."

Slocum nodded and shook the man's hand. "I'll be here in the morning for my pay, sir."

"I'll authorize it. May God go with you man."

"He might not approve of those places."

They both laughed.

After he left the headquarters, he found the washerwoman Big Madge as the sun dipped low on the Dragoons.

She looked him over and laughed. "Hell, you're crusted all over with two inches of dirt and ten pounds of horseshit."

"A bath, a shave and less talk."

"I got your other set of clean clothes."

"Good."

"Well, get you ass in here." She swept back the tent flap. "Water's hot."

He glanced as the orange ball of the sun descended. It had been over forty-eight hours since he'd slept. No wonder he was so numb. Clean, shaved, dressed in fresh clothes—he paid her and went to make camp by the springs. When he reached the spot where they always camped, he dismounted the big stout Morgan horse and picked at the still wet leathers of the cinch.

"Give me hobbles," the short Indian woman said in the darkness, holding out her hand.

Slocum shook his head and stepped over to undo the flap on his saddlebags. He drew them out and handed them to her with a rue-filled headshake. He knew who she was as she bent down to put them on the big horse—Chewy's wife.

The saddle undone, he jerked it and the Navajo blankets from the Morgan's back. She slipped the bridle off standing on her toes and then nodded to him. From her pocket she produced a slap of jerky and stuck it in his mouth before he could tell her to go.

He was too damn tired to argue. Besides, the jerky tasted fresh and not so hard it threatened to break his teeth. Not bad jerky, he decided, with the saddle on its horn and her spreading out his bedroll. Last thing he could recall that night before he passed out was shoving his dick as hard as he could into her and his testicles crying out for help when he came inside her.

Day was a purple promise when he caught the Morgan and led him to the spring. When he'd been watered, Slocum gave him a feedbag of corn and saddled him for the ride up to headquarters.

At the hitch rack he smelled the cigar smoke. Under his black felt hat, Nantan Lupan rose off the canvas chair and came to the edge of the porch. "Woolard told me you were leaving. And not saying a word to me."

"Sorry, General. I figured we'd talked all we needed the last time."

"Maybe . . ." Crook took a drag off his cigar and blew out the smoke. "How tough is this Caliche?"

"I doubt he comes out of those mountains alive."

Crook stood on edge at the porch and looked at Apache Peak, gilded in gold by the sun. "Damn, I wish you hadn't said that. Means he's going to be tough to dig out."

Slocum nodded and started up the steep steps. "Wish I could help you."

"No, you don't. You've had a bellyful of bad water, wormy rations and hard ground for a bed. I get tired of owing you for things like Diaz that the army can't seem to handle. But I'd feel ten times better if you went to Mexico with my forces."

"I ain't over losing Chako."

Crook looked back at the peak. "I understand. Just keep your head down."

"I will," Slocum said and went inside.

The officer of the day paid him a hundred and ten pesos for his pay and sixty dollars more for expenses. Slocum saluted him and picked up his money.

"Who gets Chako's pay? He have any kin?"

"Oh, yes." Slocum grinned. "Give it to Chewy's wife. She's his closest kin."

"Good."

"Not to Chewy."

"No, to his wife."

With a wave, Slocum was out the door and on the porch. General Crook was gone; only the strong smell of his cigar still lingered in the cool air. Soldiers, mule trains—the parade ground was packed with braying, cursing and the dust of many men and their animals preparing for a campaign against the broncos in the Madres.

He felt a knot behind his tongue over not going along when he turned the Morgan eastward. Be a helluva campaign—might be the last one too.

20

He arrived in Bowie at midday and went in Jenks's store. He
came from the back. "You get the word?"

Slocum shook his head. "What word?"

"Someone kidnapped Mary yesterday."

"Someone?"

"Yes." Jenks swallowed hard. "He rode in and grabbed her as
she was leaving the schoolhouse and rode off with her over his
lap. A couple of her students saw him do it."

"They know who he was?"

Jenks shook his head. "Brown horse and not much else they
could tell me. I sent word to the fort last night."

"You have any law here?"

"Just the part-time marshal. He don't have a horse. And the
sheriff is in Tucson."

"Hasn't anyone done anything?"

"I sent word to the colonel last night."

"Well, he never got it. I just came from there. Which way did
the kidnapper go?"

"West, the boys said."

"I'll go out there and look for tracks. Damn, I wish there was
someone else we could get word to about this."

"Want me to go with you? Several wanted to go after him,
but they don't have horses either."

"No. I can't find her, no one can. Damn—damn. How late yesterday?"

"Four o'clock."

"He's got a good head start. Give me some cornmeal/brown sugar mix, jerky, twenty pounds of horse corn and some hard candy."

When he started to dig out the money, Jenks waved it away. "It's our fault. We should have watched her closer. But we never expected—"

"Wasn't an Indian that took her?"

"No, he was white, those boys were certain."

Slocum gathered up the poke and the small sack of corn for the horse. "Send word to the sheriff to be on the lookout anyway."

"How can we help?" Jenks asked, sounding defeated.

Slocum looked hard at him for an answer, then at last said, "Pray."

"We will, and for you too."

"I'll sure need it," Slocum said and left the store.

At the adobe schoolhouse, two young boys joined him as he tried to decipher the tracks in the dust.

"You going after Miss Harbor's kidnapper?"

"Yes. You boys see him?"

"Ah, *sí, señor*," the Mexican boy said. "He was a *malo* hombre and hurt her and she bit him. Oh, she was *el gato bronco*, but he was stronger."

"He have a beard?"

The boys looked at each other and then shrugged. "But he wore a suit, a dusty brown one and a floppy hat," the other boy said.

Who wore a suit? A brown one. Oh, well, he probably wouldn't know who he was anyway. One thing, they had a struggle and he took her off. He gave each boy a piece of hard candy, swung up and set in to follow the few tracks he had. The worst time in his life not to have an Apache tracker—Chako or Chewy would already be in a long lope in their moccasins on his trail. All he could do was glance down as he rode and hope he had the right set.

A mile west in some tall mesquites, he found a horse pile

where the kidnapper had kept a second horse waiting, hitched to a tree. There he must have transferred her to the second one. Back in the saddle, Slocum followed the trail—Dos Cabasos lay ahead. A mining community. Chances might be he went through there. He short-loped the Morgan. He needed to take a chance and not step-by-step follow the pair, to cut down on the distance between him and them.

He didn't want to think about her spending all night with this thug. Powerful horse under him, he could cut down the time—if he hadn't wrongly guessed the outlaw's direction of travel.

When he drew close to the small business district of a few stores and a post office, he stopped to ask a bearded miner.

"A man pass through here yesterday with an attractive women?"

"Hell, mister, I ain't seen an attractive woman since I left Cripple Creek nine months ago." The man giggled at his own words.

Slocum thanked him and went on to the shabby-looking building marked BAR. He dismounted and hitched the Morgan at the rack. There was no door. Four men turned around at the bar and showed their whiskered faces to him. All were dressed like miners and wore lots of dust. They looked him over inspectively.

"I'm looking for man with an attractive woman. He would have rode through here yesterday about sundown."

"Naw, it was near dark. He didn't stay long. Bought some grub across the street. Drew a gun on some guy asked why she was gagged and tied in the saddle." The miner shook his head. "Lucky he's still alive. We all wondered about her. But none of us had horses to go after 'em."

"Which way they head?"

"Down the valley. South."

"Thanks."

"Mister, you the law?"

Slocum paused in the doorway. "I guess."

"Sure hope you find her. He's a tough one. Watch out."

"You ever see him before?"

"Yeah," another said, scratching his chin whiskers. "I seen him at the stage stop at Benson."

"You hear his name?"

"Spade, I think."

"How about Jed Slade?"

"Yeah, that's who he was. Jed Slade."

Slocum shook his head and thanked the man. Slade had her and he was headed south. Several Mormons down the valley had farms. They wouldn't tell him much—unless he found an angry polygamous wife by herself. She might. He pushed on, the sun hanging low over the Dragoons; he'd need to make as much ground as he could before sundown.

So Slade came back and got her. Must have heard about her or found her by chance—no telling. The fact he had her made it that much more urgent Slocum find them.

He stopped at a windmill and a tank to water the Morgan. The skeleton of a house was going up, with the fresh-cut framework standing. No one was about, so he watered and grained the gelding and then spread out his bedroll. Some jerky for his meal, he turned in and slept a few hours. When the moon came up, he awoke, rolled up his pallet, tossed his saddle on the Morgan and started down the valley.

Sunup he was riding by a place and saw a woman coming from a pen with a milk bucket. He turned the Morgan up the lane and nodded to her as he approached. She set down her pail and swept the loose strands of curled brown hair from her face.

"Ma'am. Did a man and woman ride by here yesterday?"

She blinked and used her hand for a shield from the sun. "I don't know."

"They were riding horses and he had her hands tied."

"Why?"

"He kidnapped her."

She dropped her gaze and shook her head.

"Thanks." He started to rein the Morgan around.

"She your woman?"

"No, she's a schoolmarm up at Bowie."

"They rode through here yesterday about noon."

"You didn't see them?" Slocum frowned at her.

"My husband did—"

"He tell you?"

"Yeah, when he came by to get my butter and eggs, he mentioned he saw a couple on his way out. He noticed her hands were tied to the saddle horn."

"Anything else?"

"No. You had breakfast?"

"No."

"I can make some if you've got time."

"I reckon I have time for that."

She smiled as if pleased. "Good. I can sure use some company."

"Your husband was here yesterday," he chided her.

"I told you why he was here—get my eggs and butter. He wasn't here twenty minutes."

"Cash crop?"

When she turned back in the doorway, her blue eyes narrowed. "And he's got him a new wife about sixteen."

"How many of you are there?" He paused to wash his hands.

"Four now."

"He tell you who that man on the road was?"

"Nope, 'cept it was strange she was tied. I figured she was some runaway wife and the guy went and got her back."

He dried his hands on the cotton-sack towel hanging there. "You considered doing it?"

"Where would I go?"

"That's up to you."

"No, it ain't. I ain't got a rig to drive out of here. No money. Not even a horse worth killing to ride. Where would I go? Work in some brothel in Tombstone?"

"Sorry," he said, seeing she was close to tears.

Not looking at him, she sniffed and busied herself on the range. "It's hell when you can't carry a baby full-term. See, all mine have died."

He nodded. "I see."

"No, you don't. Makes me fourth on the list. Now he has that new sister, she'll keep him busy."

"Anything I can do?"

She glanced back at him and then shook her head as if she'd changed her mind. "I just needed someone to complain to."

Eggs began to sizzle, and the aroma of her bacon spread to his nose. "Complain away. I can listen. Your cooking smells lovely."

"You aren't Mormon, are you?"

"Not even a jack one. Why?"

"Good," she said. "I met Hiram— Oh, I was so dumb. A real man, not a boy, finally was paying me attention. He had a neat buggy and buggy horse and took me for picnics. Oh, he had me spellbound."

She put the plate of eggs and bacon before him then used a potholder to draw out a half a pan of biscuits. "My mother warned me. Said older men were fine, but sometimes a young one would hang on longer. I wished I'd listened."

"You come from a polygamous family?"

"No. My mother and father were in love. I realize that now. Hiram Duncan ain't never been in love in his life, unless it was with himself."

"Good food," he said and nodded to the biscuit in his hand.

She smiled for the first time and her eyes sparkled. "You mean that?"

"Hey, I don't say many things I don't mean."

"You love this girl?"

"No, she's a victim. I found her in the desert six weeks ago after this man had tried to attack her. She escaped that time."

"Maybe she will this time."

"Maybe she will. I hope so. She came out here to teach, not to be abducted by someone as worthless as Jed Slade."

She cocked an eyebrow at him. "Hiram never said that's who it was."

"He knows Slade?"

"Of course. He's done business with him before."

His breakfast finished, he leaned back in the wooden chair and nodded. Slade had done lots of business in the Mormon community. His financiers for the gun deal were over at Saint David, the other settlement of saints on the San Pedro.

She straightened her back, so her breasts pushed at the dress material, and rubbed her hands on her legs under the table. The uncomfortable look on her face and the fact she chewed on her lower lip made him wonder for a moment what she wanted.

Then she began to unbutton her dress. "I don't have the body of a sixteen-year-old. But— Oh, dear God," she whispered and flung her arms around him.

A while later he swung his bare legs off the bed, rose and began to dress. "I have to find her."

"I . . . I understand," she said and swept up a wash-worn robe to wrap tight around her. Holding it hard to her body, she laughed. "Otherwise I'd tie your hands and make you stay here.'

"I may pass this way again."

"Funny, isn't it—I mean, we made love and I don't even know your name."

"Slocum."

"Alma, Alma Duncan."

"Alma Duncan, you beat any sixteen-year-old I've ever known."

She rushed over and hugged him. "Horseman, don't you ever ride by and not stop."

"I promise I won't."

She hung on his arm to the horse. He undid the reins, tightened the girth then took her in his arms and kissed her. "Alma, thanks for all your hospitality."

"You be careful—"

"I know, Slade's a killer."

She waved and he rode on.

By the prints in the dust, it seemed Slade never stayed in the Sulphur Springs community. Slocum could tell his tracks by this time without bending over. Headed south for Mexico, he guessed.

Late afternoon he approached a rancheria. He drew the Colt and checked the chambers; he didn't know this place and wanted to be ready for anything. Holstered again, he pushed the Morgan down the draw for the jacal and some pens. Many of these ranches had been abandoned in northern Sonora and on the U.S. side, because of the Apaches' bloodthirsty raids on them.

Three tough-looking men came out of the adobe house. By their hats and manner of dress he'd called them cowboys— however, none wore the red sash of Clanton's men. Slade had been there—he knew from the tracks.

A hard-eyed breed, a Mexican wearing two bandoliers and a bearded white man of ample girth. He spoke. "What'cha need?"

"I'm looking for Jed Slade." He checked the dancing Morgan under him.

"Any of you know a Jed Slade?" the big man asked the other two.

They shook their heads.

The big man threw his hands out to cover the place. "See, he ain't here."

"He was."

"You calling me a damn liar?"

Slocum shook his head. "Jed Slade rode up here with the woman he kidnapped."

"Well, I damn sure don't know Jed Slade or nothing about no kidnapped woman."

"Strange, ain't it? I been on his tracks for two days and they led right here." Slocum grasped the saddle horn in both hands and rocked back and forth to loosen his stiff back muscles.

"You the damn law?"

"No, but I'm looking for Slade."

"You may be looking for a grave."

"Mister, I can cut two of you down before the third one might get me. You're going to be the first one to die if I do. However, I'm going to excuse all that talk—where's Slade?"

"He ain't here."

It was either have a shoot-out or leave. He reached down, lifted the reins and set the Morgan to backing until he was beyond easy range. The big horse backed fast. Then Slocum saluted them and rode on. Slade had been there. He knew it. Maybe he came out on the wagon road—maybe not. No sign of his horses at the place. A mile down the road, the familiar prints in the dust gave him new hope and he set the Morgan to trotting.

By afternoon, he was deep in Sonora. Where was Slade headed? This made the second day and he felt no closer. He found a camp late in the evening. The smoke from the cooking fire carried on the wind. A man stood up with a single-shot rifle in his arms. His pregnant young woman looked up from where she squatted at her food preparation.

"*Buenas tardes,*" Slocum said, and the man nodded, still hugging the rifle. "Would you sell me some supper?"

"We have so little, but we will share it."

Slocum nodded. "I don't wish to be a burden to you."

"Get down. We eat soon."

The woman nodded in agreement.

"My name is Slocum." He stepped down and loosened the cinch. "I am looking for a man and a white woman."

"My name is Pablo. She is Nina. Such a man went by here."

"Good to meet you. How long ago?"

"Maybe a few hours. Her hands were tied." Pablo frowned, looking concerned.

"He kidnapped her three days ago from the school where she taught. Did he stop here?"

Pablo nodded. "He wanted to know how far it was to San Rico."

"Was he headed there?" Slocum squatted down on his boot heels near her small fire.

"I think so." Pablo removed his sombrero and joined him. "This woman is yours?"

Slocum shook his head. "She is a schoolteacher and came to Arizona to teach little children, not to be kidnapped and abused by worthless trash like Slade."

"This one is a bad hombre?"

"He thinks he is anyway. He sells guns and whiskey to the broncos when he isn't doing this."

"I see the evil in his eye when he was here."

"Where are you going?"

"To a rancheria. My Nina, she thinks the baby is coming, so we camp till it comes."

"Your wife?"

"No, no, she is my daughter. Her husband was killed by bandits and we only have each other."

"I have a pistol in my saddlebags. It is loaded. I have no

more caps, powder and balls for it, but I will give it to you—so you and her can be safe."

"*Gracias,*" Pablo said and she nodded with him.

"There are many bad men on the road." Then Slocum warned them to avoid the rancheria he had passed earlier.

Pablo thanked him and she fed him a bean burrito. After he ate it, he gave her two silver dollars. When she hesitated taking the money, he nodded to her belly. "For the little one."

She agreed, and Pablo grinned examining his new pistol. "*Muchas gracias, mi amigo.* May God ride with you to find her."

He trotted the big Morgan in the orange flare of sundown. San Rico was still several miles away—but chances were good that he might catch Slade there. He felt for the first time since Dos Cabasos that he had a good lead on them and a real chance to close the gap between him and them.

The moon was up when he rode into the small community under the stars. The outline of the unfinished second bell tower stood above the hovels and jacals that nested in the small valley. The long-ago builders only completed one per sanctuary, so the church stood unfinished and no taxes were due on it. The trail of missions constructed by Father Kino across Sonora to Tucson all shared that same feature.

He put the Morgan in a livery and asked about a gringo and his woman stopping there. The stable boy said he had not seen any such pair. The news was not good. Maybe Slade had contacts in this village—other saints or people he could stay with. It made sense because he could hardly take her around tied up and not draw some kind of challenge.

In the cantina, Slocum bought a drink and asked the bartender if he'd seen a gringo with a woman there that day. The barkeep called over another. He was bald-headed and an older man.

"Yes, señor. Gonzales says you ask about a white man and woman who came through here today."

"They came this way anyhow."

"Are they your amigos?"

"No. The woman is a schoolteacher and he kidnapped her."

"Oh, such a bad thing." He shook his head.

"You know where they are?"

"This hombre has a rancheria in the hills."

"Slade has a ranch down here?"

"It is not much of a ranch. A ramada, some corrals, a well and a couple of men to guard it."

"From what?"

"We don't know. But his pistoleros are cheap ones." The man looked around, then, satisfied there was not danger in continuing, put his forearms on the bar. "He may deal in stolen horses—maybe he sells some *putas*—something, we think. You know?"

"Yes, he's not worth shooting." Was he fixing to sell Mary? "Where does he sell these women?"

"On the border." The man shrugged. "They are captured Indian girls mostly and they don't bring much. They bring them to him and he sells them to the brothels."

"Where would he sell a white woman?"

"Oh, she would bring many pesos."

"Where?"

"Maybe Guaymos or Mexico City."

"Can I hire a guide to show me where his rancheria is?"

"Franco," he said and waved a young man over from a side table. When he came, the man put his arm on the younger one's shoulder and talked softly. Franco looked up, met Slocum's gaze and nodded.

"When do you wish to go there?" the man asked.

"Tonight."

"Franco will show you. He is a good man."

"Yes, *gracias*," Slocum said and downed the mescal he had ordered. He and his guide left the cantina and went for his horse.

"I have no *caballo*, señor."

"We can ride him double. You're small."

The Morgan out and saddled, they rode him from the village under the stars. Franco pointed the way and they soon went into some hills. They left the Morgan hitched to a mesquite in a side canyon, then climbed a steep hillside to spy down on the dark cluster of pens and a ramada.

"I can pay you now," Slocum said in whisper, holding his Winchester.

"No, señor. I can go with you and help get her free."

"There might be shooting."

"I have no gun."

"Can you use one?"

"Ah, *sí, señor*."

He handed him his Colt. "Don't shoot me or her. The rest are expendable."

"I don't savvy that word."

"Means you can shoot them."

Franco's teeth shone in the night with his pleased grin. "Fine pistol."

"Come on, we've got work to do."

They crossed the open flats in the starlight and reached the pens. The horses grunted in their sleep as they eased around the pen. He sent Franco the other way. Where was she?

He moved across the open spot and reached the shadowy, dark ramada— Someone smashed him in the back of his head and his knees buckled. Then it all went blank.

21

Slocum could only see out of one eye. But he could see Franco, his head bowed, tied to an opposite post of the ramada. Like Slocum, he too was bound with his back to the post. Who'd hit him?

No one in sight. His head hurt all the way through. The sun was up, so Slocum had no idea how long he'd been unconscious. Had they been tied up and abandoned? No telling. The big thing was getting free and after Slade. Whew, the pounding at his temples was bad.

"Franco," he hissed.

The youth raised his head and nodded.

"Who did this?"

"Slade's men. They must have got word we were coming, huh?"

"I didn't tell them." Slocum tried to clear his head. "Is she with them?"

"There was a gringo woman with them."

"Her hands tied?"

"I think so. She looked very tired." Franco shook his head in disgust.

"Damn, she probably is. Who told them we were coming?"

"I wish I knew. I'd kick their asses in."

He strained at his hands. If they managed to get loose—they had no money, no guns and no sign of the Morgan or any horses in the pens. Be damn hard to chase them down in that shape. But he'd have to.

"You getting loose?"

"Ah, *sí*, a little more, señor." Franco was really straining.

"Good. Mine ain't giving."

It was the braying of a jackass coming into the camp to find his horse friends that made Slocum whirl around. He pulled hard on the ropes cutting his wrists—they gave a little, but he knew the sticky feeling—that was his blood. How long would it take him to get to Guaymos on a burro?

"I am free, señor."

"Good. Help me."

Franco soon had him loose and was rubbing his own wrists.

"Why didn't he kill us?" Slocum asked.

"I don't know. The woman, she cried I think was why. He was afraid she would tell they had shot us too."

"How long have they been gone?"

"Oh, hours, señor. Where do you go now?"

"I want that burro to ride."

"Ride a burro with no guns after those bandits?" The young man looked shocked.

"I've done worse, Franco." He slid the corral bars in place and smiled at the captive gray donkey. "Worst part, I can't pay you. They've taken most all of my money."

"Oh, señor, I don't need money. I am *mucho* grateful to be alive and free."

"Alive and free is nice. They leave any food?" Slocum was looking around for a bridle and possibly a pad.

"I don't know. Ah, here are some frijoles in this pot," he said over his discovery.

"Good. We can feast on cold frijoles, huh?"

"Oh, they have been burned."

"We'll feast on burnt ones then."

"Señor Slocum, may I go with you to Guaymos?"

He blinked at the youth. "Why?"

"I may never get to go there if I don't go with you."

"Well, we have a knife in this boot they didn't find," Slocum said, pulling up his pant leg. Then, lifting the other one, he drew out a small .31-caliber revolver. "This and that jackass, we may make it there."

They both laughed.

As they sat on the ground sharing the scorched beans with crudely whittled wooden spoons, burro number two came braying off the hillside. A white one. Slocum shook his head and grinned at Franco. "There's our other steed."

Franco laughed at the notion. "I never had so much fun in my life, and it is so serious. I mean the señorita and all."

"Sometimes when things get the blackest all you can do is laugh."

"I never knew such a man as you."

"Good thing there aren't more," Slocum said. "Let's catch Snowball and get on our way. Jed Slade, we're coming after you."

Forced to keep his boot toes up or snag them on the ground, he beat a tattoo with a stick on the gray one's butt to keep him trotting. So they hurried uphill and down and across the desert until they came to a small village that looked golden-walled in the setting sun.

"What is this place?" Franco asked when they reined up.

"I hope Horseville," Slocum said. He jumped off his burro, pulled his pants out of his crotch and led the animal with a stiff limp toward the gate.

They found the stable man and awoke him from a long siesta in a hammock. He looked them up and down doubtfully as he set his legs over the side.

"We need two horses."

The man shook his head. "I don't have them."

"What do you have we can ride?"

"Mules."

Slocum considered the man as he ran his fingers through his hair. He went to the corral and studied the hipshot, sleepy-looking mules. About twelve hands high, they would be much better than the burros. "They broke to ride?" He turned back for the answer.

"Some. They will beat those burros."

"Some saddles?"

The man nodded.

"How much?"

"Twenty pesos for two."

"Ten."

"Fifteen."

"Twelve."

"Fourteen is my last offer."

Slocum nodded and sat on the ground. He pulled off his boots and found the paper money in the walletlike slit. "We want them saddled in the morning before daylight."

"All right," the man grumbled.

"Oh, you can have them two burros in trade. They're well broke." Slocum pointed to the cantina and clapped his man on the shoulder, raising a cloud of dust. "Food is next."

"I hope the beans aren't burned this time."

Slocum nodded, looked around, adjusted the small handgun in his waistband and went inside. The place was dimly lighted by some candles. A short woman came over with a low-cut blouse and looked at them with her dark eyes as if eyeing the size of their business. "Ah, hombres, what do you want?"

"Some good food, some mescal and who knows," Slocum said and nodded to the bartender.

She caught him by the arm. "I have the pussy when you are ready."

Slocum nodded and winked at Franco. The youth about blushed, but he nodded to him.

"Oh, we can feed you some *cabrito*—it is very tender."

"*Cabrito* sounds great. Bring it on."

Franco nodded, and they sat at the table in front of the empty bar and sipped the mescal the bartender brought to them. Soon the woman, called Cyd, brought them steaming goat meat and black beans on a wooden tray.

"Who do I get to feed?" she asked.

"Set in his lap," Slocum said and raised his glass in toast. "To our new mules!"

Cyd made herself at home in the boy's lap, feeding him fingers full of the moist meat and then wiping his lips with a napkin with much care and fuss. Franco looked a little uncomfortable at all the attention. Slocum winked at him and dug in on his own. His backbone was gnawing on his navel again. The food was good, and when he finally sat back and looked across at them, he saw she had poor Franco worked up.

"Better take him to your casa," Slocum said to her and slid a silver half dollar across the table. "That's for all night."

"Ah, *sí*." She dropped the coin between her breasts and hustled the youth to his feet. They soon disappeared out the back door.

Slocum leaned back. "A white man, some pistoleros and a white lady pass through here today?" he asked the bartender.

He nodded, coming over to refill his glass.

"They say where they were going?"

"No."

"You know them?"

"One pistolero they call Blanco."

"He an albino?"

"Ah, *sí*. White hair, silver eyes."

"How many pistoleros?"

"Two."

"Three men?"

The barkeep shook his head. "Two gringos, two Mexicans."

Slocum nodded. Thorpe must have joined them somewhere. Maybe he had been at this place where they kept their stolen horses and slave *putas*. Slocum would know three of them on sight anyway. But sipping the fiery mescal, he felt the most regret about Mary's plight and not being able to get her out of it sooner.

Predawn came early. The mules saddled and bridled with curb bits, they slung their heads and acted bad enough that Slocum knew they weren't dead broke. He held a twisted ear while Franco got on, and when he let go, the show was on. The mule crow-hopped across the square in the shadowy light. Then he got real stiff-legged and pitched Franco off.

No time for bronc mules to act up. Slocum ran and caught him. Held the headstall hard to his knee as the mule snorted fire and tried to circle away from him. The mule continued to go around with his head tight to Slocum's leg. Loose at last, he ducked his nose between Slocum's knees, but by then Slocum was beating his tender flank underneath with a cross-over back-and-forth swing of the thick rope reins. The mule soon jerked his head up and began a stiff-legged run around the square, braying in protest.

"Give me the lead on that other one," Slocum shouted, and Franco rushed in his mount and took it. Then with mule *numero dos* dallied up to his leg, Slocum shook his boot out of the left stirrup.

"Step up on mine, then drop into your saddle," Slocum said to Franco in the midst of all the mule honking. "He can't buck with his nose in my lap."

The youth was like a cat getting in the saddle. But while Dos couldn't buck, he kicked a hole in the air behind his heels. Slocum paid his flying hooves no mind. He adjusted the gun in his waistband, held the dally tight and waved to the smiling Cyd on the porch. They left out of the square on two mules walking on eggs.

It was a mile or so of greasewood flats before the mules settled down. Slocum tossed the lead at Franco and Dos spooked back, but the boy made him get right back up beside Slocum in his trot.

"They'll be broke by the time we get there," Franco said and laughed. "I didn't think we'd ever get them so we could ride them."

"We had no time for nonsense. Man, a damn bunch of wild horses or mules like these just needs to be contained and then ride the fire out of them."

Slocum twisted in the sorry, mostly wooden Mexican saddle and saw nothing on the heat wave–dazzled flats they'd crossed. Their new mounts still beat burros, but they were stiff-legged trotting. He pushed his shoulder back against the sore muscles in his back. *We're coming, Mary.*

22

Late in the afternoon, they reached San Phillipe, another mission on the Kino Trail. Slocum found enough money to buy the mules each a morral of corn. They hooked them over their heads, and the two of them ate with an older street vendor. Squatted there in the day's still heat, her food was rewarding after the long ride.

The about toothless woman had seen the pistoleros and the white woman pass through with two gringos. Maybe two hours before them, but she shook her head when Slocum asked where they went or if they had stayed in the village.

"We can check around," he said to Franco when they finished eating. "Be careful. They know you now."

"Ah, *sí*, and I know them."

The mules hobbled at the edge of the village in a dry wash, Slocum and Franco split up to see if they could find the kidnappers, promising to meet in the alley after making a round. In an hour Slocum was back without learning a thing. He heard someone in the dark, hurrying up the alley, and his hand went to the gun butt. Then an out-of-breath Franco hissed at him.

"I found the two—Blanco and the other one. They never saw me. They are with a *puta* at her jacal. Pretty drunk."

"Good job. We better get those two. See my horse?"

Franco shook his head. "There are no horses there."

They hurried down the alley, keeping their profiles low.

When they approached the jacal, a dog went to barking. Would that warn the pair? A woman came out and cussed at the dog. He quit barking and they went on. Franco pointed out the adobe building with the light behind the closed curtain. "That's the place."

"Find a club. Go by the back door. One runs out, hit him over the head."

"I savvy. You be careful."

Slocum nodded that he heard him and moved to reach the front door. Easing his way, he listened.

"Ah, *mi amigo*," a drunk voice said. "You screw her like a rabbit. Give her all of it."

Perhaps if they were that involved in an orgy . . . Beside the open door, smelling the bitter gunsmoke stink from the small pistol near his face, he could hear the fierce grunting and the other one cheering him on.

"Hands high!" he shouted as he swept the curtain aside.

The dark-faced one whirled and his hand went for the pistol. Slocum aimed and shot him in the face. The lights went out. Slocum could see the snowy-bodied one, who was using the screaming whore doggy style when he dove for his gun in the bitter cloud of gunsmoke that boiled up in the room. Slocum fired twice and the albino lay still.

Slocum stepped back, and the sobbing, screaming *puta* crawfished away from him.

He told her to shut up and light some candles. Coughing on the acrid smoke, he squatted to find the dark-faced one's gun. It was his own he discovered when he had it in his hand and the candle lighted the room.

She wrapped herself and backed to the wall, looking in horror at him. Franco came in with a club and she sucked in her breath and trembled.

"He's with me." Slocum jerked his gun belt off the outlaw. "See how much of my money Whitey has on him and get his gun and holster set."

Franco nodded.

"Where are the others staying?" Slocum asked her.

"I don't know." She clutched her hands and elbows together

in prayer fashion, and her lips mumbled, "Hail Mary, Mother of God . . ."

"Where did you find them?"

"They came to me."

"You know them?"

She shook her head; the limp hair fell in her face and she did nothing about it.

"The men kidnapped a woman. There are two more?"

She shuddered and slid down the wall to a pile on the floor. "I am a poor *puta*. I kidnap no one." She began to cry.

"Where did they stay?"

"Maybe in a casa." She snuffed her nose and sobbed.

"Which one?"

"At the edge of town—a white one beside the road."

"Can you show us?"

"You can find it." She pointed south. "You can't miss it."

"Who owns this casa?"

She swallowed hard and managed. "Delo Mannas."

"Who's that?"

"A big man—many ranches—much money."

"Franco, you ever hear of him?"

Franco wore the albino's gun belt and handed Slocum a fistful of gold coins. "I never heard of him. But I travel nowhere."

"That's the money they took from me." Slocum shook his head—most of it was there. "I guess they never shared it with Slade."

"Slade?" she asked and she looked around like one did for a buzzing rattler.

"You know him?"

"He is *malo hombre*. He is here?"

"These men worked for him."

She looked at the two and shook her head. "I didn't know that."

"This casa is a short ways from here?" Slocum asked.

She nodded. "It is big white house."

"They came on foot?"

"*Sí*, they walked by here. I see them from the door and I say, 'Are you lonely?' They say yes. I tell them to come in." She shrugged.

"You ever see them before?"

"No."

"We better go see this Mannas. Maybe he can tell us more."
Franco agreed.

"Here's ten pesos. They don't need a fancy funeral."

"Funeral? Me? I cannot stay here with dead men—alone."
She looked bewildered.

"You can take care of it for that much money. Come on,
Franco, we need to see this Mannas."

"Don't leave them here!" she shrieked after them, but
Slocum and the boy were already running out the door and
down the alley. "Come back!"

A block away from her place, Slocum slowed to a jog and
tried to see the "big casa" in the starlight.

"It must be down here," he said, looking through the lacy
mesquites.

"Why does rich man live here?" Franco asked. "This town is
so poor."

"He must own some ranches nearby—" Slocum stopped and
pointed out the two-story building. Some lights shone in the
windows and a lamp was lit out in front. Slocum skirted some
tall pancake cactus and Spanish daggers and headed for the
front door.

"Keep an eye out," he said and went on.

His rap on the carved wooden door was loud. He stood back
a few feet, hand on his gun butt, expecting anything. The door
opened and a dark-eyed woman told him good evening in a
smoky voice. She wore a filmy dress and her cleavage caught
the refection of light on her high-rise breasts.

He swept off his hat. "Señor Mannas here?"

She shook her head. "Can I help you, señor?"

"You are his señora?"

She smiled like that was out of the question. "I am his servant."

Slocum tried to see beyond her. "And Señor Slade, I can
speak to him?"

"No, you just missed him. Señor Slade rode away a short
time ago."

"Did the señor ride with him?"

She smiled. "No, he went earlier to a ranch where there has been a death."

"Why did Señor Slade leave this time of night?"

She shook her head. "I have no idea."

"Did he take Señorita Harbor with him?"

"Who?"

"The woman he kidnapped in Arizona."

"I must close this door, señor—"

Slocum stepped up and braced it half-open. "He came here to sell her to Mannas, didn't he?"

"I know nothing." She backed away and shook her head, looking frightened.

Slocum took on the offense and came in the entryway. "No, you know. He brought the woman here to sell her to Mannas. Where did they go?"

"I don't know—"

"Yes, you do." He caught her by the arm and pulled her close to his face. Close enough he could smell her expensive perfume and the musk of her body. "Didn't he come to sell the woman to him?"

"Y-yes—" She went limp in his hands, knees buckled; she fainted. He was forced to sweep her up in his arms. In the living room he carried her to a couch and laid her down.

"Did Mannas buy her?"

"No—" she managed, holding her wrist over her eyes. "He had left for the ranch before they came."

"Why did Slade and Thorpe run off?"

"They heard someone was in the village asking questions about them."

Slocum shook his head and grinned down at her. "You told them that lie, didn't you?"

"She was very pretty." Looking pale, she raised up on her elbows.

"Very pretty. Where're they going?"

"They rode south. Is she yours?"

"My worry. Yes. Did Slade ride a big Morgan horse out of here?"

"I think so. He left some horses in the stables for his men to ride when they came back."

"They won't need them. They stole mine."

She shrugged.

"Good evening. I am sorry I upset you." He turned and crossed the tile floor.

"Señor," she called out when he reached the doorway.

He paused and looked back at her.

"I feel very bad for her. I once was kidnapped."

Slocum nodded and went outside. Franco was there. "We need to get their horses out of the barn, get the mules and head south."

"How long ago did they leave?" Franco asked.

"A few hours ago." Slocum looked at the stars. *We're coming, Mary.*

23

The dusty road to Guaymos was cluttered with two-wheel *carettas* loaded with unginned cotton, raw strong-smelling wool, hay, firewood sticks and produce: melons, ear corn and some citrus. Their dry axles squeaked so loud they could be heard for miles, as the thin, white oxen pulled them along at a snail's pace. Now and then there was a pinto yoke or a black span—but most were white, the color of the dust that boiled up from Slocum and Franco's horses' and the two mules' hooves.

Sparse, mostly dead trees lined the King's Highway, the Camino Real—turkey buzzards sat like onlookers along the route. Dead draft animals beside the tracks furnished enough nourishment; they spent most of their days on a limb, crapping giant white streaks on everything under them. In early morning and before sundown they hopped down to the nearest source, and after eating the eyes out of the newest one, they jumped around, balanced by their great wings, to the dead one's belly. There they could easily tear open the thinner hide and expel the sour gases as they feasted on *ala viscera*. Squawking and quarrelsome they kept the ravens run off, and the mangy coyotes, until they'd had their gastronomic fill. Then, flapping their wings, they went back to their special roosts to preen their black feathers.

If a coyote really challenged them, they vomited enough sour-smelling puke on his head that he fled to escape the horror

of it. His eyes and nose on fire, he ran whining to hide, to paw
away at the stinging, stinking mess for hours. Only the larger
harpy eagles could run the vultures off. More athletic and
shorter tempered, they could scream, hold their wings out and
look big as horses to send the vultures away. When no live game
existed for them, the harpies shared the road carrion.

Broken-down wagons and *carettas* lined the road. Great
wooden wheels splinted and broken, *caretta* parts, boards,
rails—they made the fuel for night fires if they could be hacked
off. Or a fire was started in the center and the wheel burned all
night to reach the edge; some still smoldered a day later.

Here and there several freight wagons were lashed together
and pulled by twenty teams of stout oxen, rolled up the road.
Usually they had armed guards on horseback, for their freight
was of more value than farm goods and they traveled in trains of
several. The teamsters walking beside these long lines of draft
animals used bullwhips and loud commands. They were tough
and looked hard-eyed from under their high-peaked sombreros,
with disgust at the peons and their two-wheeled conveyances.

Burro trains brought cooking wood. Each animal bristling
with sticks like a huge pile of dead brush on the move, they
stayed in line without halter or lead. Single file, they went beside the tracks. If one broke the formation, the driver com-
manded a fast dog to rush in, bite its heels and put it back in
line. Even a small colt trailing his mother had to obey the road
rule or feel the wrath of the dog's sharp teeth—and quick-like
the colt learned the ways.

Men, boys and dogs herded small herds of sheep and goats
for the meat market. They too stayed in close-knit formation,
flowing like a blanket as they went to meet the butcher. Sometimes a faster moving carriage or buggy pulled by fine horses
would be held up by such a flock, and the driver issued many
bad words as to the herder's ancestry for blocking his way.

In mid-afternoon, when such a luxurious conveyance went
by Slocum, he noticed the fine-looking señorita behind the
black lace fan in the coach window. Her raven black hair was
piled on top of her head and spilled down the back in great long
curls. Dark eyes, big as saucers, long alluring lashes, a slender

nose and lips like fresh rose petals to kiss, she sat up straight-backed as her grandmama had always insisted. Under the black veil she had pulled back to expose her face was one of Mexico's finest examples of womanhood—he knew it without even speaking a word to her. They were all starved vixens in a fluffy featherbed—torrid lovers that could waste a strong man. Then when it was over they would liquidly squirm on their backs, pointing their rock-hard nipples at the ceiling, turning up the edge of their haughty mouths in a half sneer and challenging him for more. He nodded to her—Mexico's finest.

Three hard-faced pistoleros rode in the rear of the polished coach. Dressed in buckskin coats and pants, they wore criss-crossed ammo belts and each carried two six-guns, a big knife and a new repeater in his saddle scabbard. Their sombrero's chin straps drawn under hard-set jaws, they all three rode good barb horses—not mustangs. They trotted forty feet behind the coach as if in military formation. The protectors of her unfractured hymen, they also kept her from harm's way. They would die before anyone touched her with bad intent. Like the sharp-toothed dog that kept the burros and sheep in line, these men kept the world away from their patron's daughter.

"You see her?" Franco asked aghast as the coach moved on with the sheep band cleared from the road.

"Pretty young woman," Slocum said and nodded his head, reining the bay horse around the bleating mass.

"Oh, she looked like an angel. Who was she?"

"Easy, my friend. She's from a very rich family, the Peraltas—that was the family crest on the coach door. A poor farm boy from the sticks would not stand a chance with the likes of her."

"I don't care. I want her."

"Easy, amigo. You see those three pistoleros riding guard. They'd kill you like an ant if you even spoke to her."

"I'd die with a smile on my face."

"Hell, there's all kinds of pussy in Mexico. Some ain't that pretty, but it really is all good."

"I would marry her."

"Franco. You won't ever see her again. Thank the good Lord you even had a chance to peek at her today."

"I want her for my wife."

"People want icebergs for their beer too and they don't get them in Mexico."

"I could show her I was a man."

"Damn, boy, you got plumb intoxicated with one look."

Franco nodded his head and booted his roan horse in a trot. "Come on. We need to find this Mary Harbor so I can go find my angel."

Slocum shook his head and wondered how to bring that boy out of the clouds. Guaymos blushed with business. The streets were clogged, so getting around was like being in a labyrinth, pushing their horses around and then back. Youths hurried alongside their stirrups offering them all the services, including pussy. Franco shook his head as if to clear it.

"Things are very hectic here."

"Everyone wants your money." Slocum smiled at him and booted the bay past a stalled *caretta*.

"I have no money."

"You have a gun. You ride a horse and lead a mule."

"But I can barely ride him and could not hit a bull in the ass with this pistol."

"To them, you are a man of substance. No! No!" Slocum said, sharp enough they could understand as a new wave of these juvenile pimps rushed out to offer them the services of some *puta*.

"Look," Franco pointed. "The Morgan horse, no?"

A cold chill ran down Slocum's sun-blazed cheeks. The Morgan horse and two others were hitched at a rack before the Imperial Hotel. He stepped down and handed the reins to Franco. "Stay with them and close by."

"You need me?"

"I need you to watch these horses and mules. If they come out, follow them. I'll find you later."

"What if—"

"What if they kill me?"

Franco swallowed and nodded.

"You figure out a way to get her away from them?" Slocum asked.

"I will, but let nothing happen to you, *mi amigo*."

Slocum nodded that he heard him.

In the shadowy lobby, he nodded to the clerk, took the register and twisted it around. "Jed Slade" was written in fresh ink.

"What room?" He stabbed at the name with his index finger.

"Room two." With wide eyes, and all the cords in his neck exposed, the clerk tossed his head toward the stairs.

Slocum nodded and took them two at a time. Six-gun in his hand on the top flight, he headed for the door marked two. His ear close to the thin wood, he heard Slade say, "We need to sell her and get—"

Slocum's boot mashed open the door. Mary screamed. Slocum's six-gun spoke with an ear-shattering explosion, and Slade drew up when the bullet struck him in the chest. The room boiled with bitter gunsmoke. Thorpe raised his hands and cried out, "No!"

Slocum held his second shot. Mary rushed to him, and he hugged her with his left arm.

"Oh, I thought they'd killed you." She sobbed on his shirt.

"Thorpe, get over here." Slocum motioned with his gun muzzle. Still holding her with his left arm, he holstered his own gun and jerked Thorpe's out.

"Start downstairs. Thorpe, you make a move and you're going to be as dead as he's going to be." He indicated the fallen Slade.

"How did you find us?"

"The horse."

"I told him that damn fancy horse would be our ruin. No, he had to have him."

"You'll have plenty of time to think about that horse in prison. Get going."

"I was so afraid they had killed you." She shook her head and had wet eyes.

"No, they just left us to die." He showed her the door and they went down the stairs.

"Señor—" the frightened clerk started.

"Send an undertaker upstairs; his business is going to improve." Slocum motioned for Thorpe to go on to the front door.

The youth swallowed and nodded.

Franco shouted from horseback, "I am here! You have her!"

Slocum nodded. "I'll take the Morgan. Here," he said to Mary. "I'll help you onto the—"

Thorpe used the opportunity to turn and run. Slocum scowled and drew his gun. Too many people for him to chance a shot. Damn. "Never mind him. We need to move on." He holstered his gun and boosted her into the saddle.

Then, catching the third one's reins, he mounted the Morgan and tossed his head. "Let's get out of here." He had no desire to explain it all to the *policía*.

They moved at a slow pace through traffic that made him anxious, until he pointed to a side street. The dirt way led down into a draw and he turned them up the sandy base. He pointed to a tall gate.

"Ring the bell, Franco." He nodded to reassure her. Her face looked sun-blistered and her hair a mess. Maybe she was worse off than he'd first thought.

"Señor?" a burly man asked, opening the gate.

"Tell Don Marino that Slocum is here with guests."

The man squinted as if to be certain who he saw and then bowed. "He is always glad to see his amigo Slocum."

Slocum nodded to Mary and smiled as he booted the Morgan for the open gate. "We have a sanctuary."

Don Marino rushed down the stairs covered in red bougainvilleas. The short, white-headed man smiled and held out his arms. "So long you have been away."

Slocum hugged the man in the impeccable white suit. "It has been a while. Señor, this is Señorita Mary Harbor. Some bandits kidnapped her in Arizona. Franco, my man, and I have been on their trail for many days."

"You are very fortunate, my dear. Rest at my humble house and get your strength back. Lupe! Lupe!" he called out, and a handsome woman in her thirties came to the head of the stairs.

"Lupe, help this dear girl."

"Ah, *sí*," she said and hurried down the steps to take Mary in her care.

"You'll be fine with her," Slocum told her, and she agreed,

still looking concerned as she went off with the woman chattering to her.

The stable boys were gathering reins to lead off the many animals.

"Watch that mule," Slocum warned one of them. "He kicks."

Don laughed. "You get her kidnappers."

"I shot one in the hotel. The other got away. I didn't need to talk to the *policía*."

"I will talk to them. Who is this other one?"

"Thorpe, a gringo."

Don nodded. "He won't get far. Come, you two. We can offer you a bath and some clean clothes, or have you eaten?"

"We can wait to eat," Slocum said, and Franco agreed, looking around awed at the luxury of the place.

"This is the sort of place where she lives?" Franco asked him.

"The Peralta girl?"

"*Sí*."

"Yes. See what I mean?"

"Oh, yes."

Slocum shook his head. The vision of her wasn't out of the boy's head. It might never leave either. He hoped Mary's condition improved; she had looked so tired when Lupe led her away.

Don Marino handled the *policía*, and the lieutenant, who came to his house, promised that if Thorpe was in the city, they would find him. He shook their hands and left.

Slocum, Franco and their host sat on the sunny patio and sipped drinks. Feeling clean for the first time in weeks, Slocum enjoyed the rest and relaxation in his starched clothing. Her hair washed and rolled, the dirt gone from her face, her blistered cheeks and lips healing with Lupe's cream, Mary returned to them. Some of the spirit in her footfall Slocum recalled from when she walked toward him that first day.

"The broncos? Will you Americans crush them?" the don asked as he poured more whiskey in their glasses.

"Crook is the man." Slocum nodded. "He knows how to do it."

"Good. I have some mines in the Madres. Broncos have cost me much money and lives."

"Your mines will be fine when Crook gets through. Our horses are rested and so is she. We need to head home. I want to sell one of the mules and the extra horses."

"My man will handle it for you." The don offered them cigars. Franco waved away his offer.

Don Marino smiled at him. "You are not over this girl yet?"

Franco smiled and shook his head.

"I was like that at your age."

"Did you get her, señor?"

"Oh, no, but it made me rich trying to win her hand."

Franco frowned. "Were you sad?"

"About her making me be rich? No."

They all laughed.

Later Slocum spoke to Mary. "We need to go back."

She nodded and wet her lip. "They have been very nice to me here. But I want to go back and teach my children. I will always owe them. When should we leave?"

"Tomorrow."

"Fine." She dropped her gaze. "How will I ever repay you?"

"You have no debt to me."

Blinking her eyes, she raised her face and looked at him. "Twice you came and saved my life."

"You owe me nothing. I'm pleased you're getting stronger."

"Oh, I will be fine. I also have a sombrero Lupe insists I wear home."

"Get it out. We leave at daybreak."

"I will thank Don Marino for all his hospitality too."

"He is pleased you're better."

"Slocum—" She took both his hands in hers and backed away until they were apart. "I will be ready."

He nodded and closed his eyes. The dream. She was leaving him like she did in the dreams. What did it mean? He watched her hurry down the hallway, lithe again on her feet. It roiled his guts to see her disappear into her room. Only a *bruja* would know the future.

24

They left Guaymos in the shadowy night, the streets crowded with water vendors, herds of milk goats with the white stuff only a pull on a teat away, firewood-laden burros, and *carettas* with swinging carcasses of freshly butchered heading for the market. They wound their way through the traffic, Slocum on the Morgan, her on a fancy dish-faced sorrel mare, a gift of the don, and Franco on his roan, leading Uno with their camping things and food.

The road north was crowded with two-way traffic, and they were forced to go around many slow vehicles and trains. As the day began to heat up, they kept their horses in a long trot, a sustainable pace to make many miles before they needed to stop for the night.

"We can reach the village of Bath by nightfall," Slocum told her, riding stirrup to stirrup with her. "We can get a room there."

"That would be fine. I don't need a room."

"We have four more long days."

She smiled. "I'll be fine and grateful to be home."

Bath was a small village with a church, but the town was a busy place. Slocum noted the bustling activity when they rode in.

"Fiesta?" Franco asked.

Slocum shrugged. He booted his horse over and asked a man leading a burro with water jugs. "What is happening here?"

"A grand wedding, Don Peralta's daughter, Maria Anita Consuela Peralta, is marrying Don Leguna."

Slocum nodded and rode back. "A daughter of Peralta is marrying some Don Leguna."

Franco frowned. "You think it is her?"

"Who?" Mary asked.

"A young woman Franco loves."

"Oh."

Slocum said, "He's never met her. Only seen her in a coach."

Mary smiled at back at Franco and nodded in approval, then turned to the front and rode on. Slocum glanced aside as they passed a cantina. Two men that wore red sashes around their waists loafed on the porch.

"What is wrong?" Mary asked as they rode up the street.

"Nothing."

"You look concerned."

Slocum dismissed it—still, the red sashes could mean that old man Clanton's men were in town or up to something. Clanton and the Peraltas were longtime enemies over the stock rustling business.

Franco came up on his left side. "Can we stay for the wedding?"

Slocum turned to her.

"I would love to see such a rich thing." Mary smiled at them.

"Fine. If it is tomorrow, we can watch it."

"Good," Franco said. "Could I give her away?"

They laughed, and Slocum found the small rooming house where he took rooms and they put their animals up in a nearby pen. After they unsaddled and unpacked, Franco put morrals with corn in them over their heads.

A street vendor served them food as the sun sank. Mary looked fine after the hard ride. And Slocum had found out that the wedding would be at nine in the morning. But he noticed another red sash among the people walking about. After he took Mary to her room and said good night, he told Franco to watch her.

"Is there something wrong?"

"Too many of Clanton's cowboys are here for it to be a coincidence."

"What can we do?"

"I don't know. I will try to learn something."

"If I can help—"

"Watch Mary."

"I will."

Slocum made his way in the shadows. He drank cerveza in the back of the cantina, then slipped like smoke out the back door again. There were close to a dozen of the Clanton bunch. They drank in silence, slant-eyed and tough. Most were Mexicans, though Slocum knew several of Clanton's rustlers were Texans. He circled the village and found the camp of Peralta—armed camp and guarded. Many tents and a busy place as the wedding drew closer and people scurried to ready everything. Slocum slipped away into the night and crossed the small hill. He stopped short at the snort of a horse.

This gathering of men in the night was for one purpose. He didn't need to see their sashes. They planned to storm the Peralta camp. Why? Old man Clanton had some revenge plan, and the heart of it might lie with the Peralta daughter. If he had time, he'd get their horses and a spare. Maybe the three of them could sweep her out. Clanton wanted revenge for some reason—kidnapping the daughter might be the key to all of this.

Away at last from the converging army, he ran on his boot soles. Out of breath, he slipped into the rooming house, and not seeing Franco, he rapped on her door.

"Yes?"

"Slocum."

"I'm coming," she said and unlocked the door to let him in.

"Have you seen Franco?" he asked.

She was buttoning her dress. "No. Why?"

"Clanton's bunch, I think, intends to kidnap the Peralta girl."

"Oh, no. What can we do?" She tugged on the dress to straighten it.

"Get her out of harm's way."

"What's wrong?" Franco busted in the room.

"The Peralta girl must be what they want."

"So?"

Slocum looked hard at the youth. "It may take some straight shooting to get her out."

Franco nodded. "I can try."

"No try—we will only have one shot in most cases."

"I savvy."

"It will be dangerous for you," he said to Mary.

"Those men won't treat her nice," Franco said.

"No, nor you if we fail."

"I will go with you," she said. "I'll help do what I can."

They rushed out, saddled the horses and tossed the packs on the mule. When they were ready to go, Slocum led the way and they wound out of a dry wash and circled back of the village. He wanted to come out beyond Clanton's men and enter the camp before they attacked it.

Distant shots shattered the night. Slocum reined up. Too late, he whirled the Morgan and set out for the hill between them and the camp. On the rise he dismounted and jerked the Winchester out.

"Mary, stay with the horses over this hill. If we need you, I'll shout your name, and come on the double."

Slocum, accompanied on his heels by the youth, hurried down the hill. He carried the rifle in his hands ready for anything. The gunshots sounded more sporadic. They rounded a tent, and a horseman brandishing a pistol rode right on them. Slocum dropped to his knee and shot him.

Franco caught his spooked horse.

"Hitch him," Slocum said and hurried toward the main part. He noticed a man raping a woman on the ground. He struck him in the back of his head with his gun butt. The rapist pitched forward. Then Slocum jerked the woman to her feet. "Where is she at?"

Too numb to answer him, she pressed down her skirt.

"Peralta's daughter. Where is she? We need to get her out of here."

"Come," she said.

Slocum waved Franco on. More shooting in the other part of the camp. At the fancy coach, the woman opened the door, keeping low.

"Maria," she called out softly.

Wrapped in a blanket, someone appeared on her knees.

"We are amigos. You must go with us," Slocum said. "It's not safe here."

"But my guards . . ."

"They may be dead," Slocum said, on the lookout for any of Clanton's men.

"He saved me, Maria. He is not with these bandits."

"All right."

"Franco, take the women to the horses. I'll cover you."

"*Sí.* Come this way," Franco said and hurried them for the horse and the tent.

Three men on foot came running. Slocum took aim at their outlines from the light of the tents on fire behind them. He saw their Texas hats and opened fire with the rifle. His bullets stopped them. He retreated to some barrels, hoping by then Franco had the women on horseback.

A surge of pistol-firing riders came around the camp from his left. He emptied the rifle into them, knocking down two horses and causing a collision. The Winchester empty, he dropped it and drew his .44. He edged for the tent, drawing some fire, but it was more like scattered shots. Around the tent, he rushed to the hilltop. He looked up, and Mary came over the crest, on the fly with his Morgan, sliding both horses to a stop.

"The others gone?" he asked, out of breath.

"Yes."

"Good. Ride out of here," he said and bounced off his right boot and into the saddle.

In two jumps, the big horse was beside her and they were off, crossing the greasewood scrub desert under the stars. They soon joined the other three as they swung north. The woman he'd saved was riding the Clanton horse. The Peralta girl clung to Franco's waist, looking back with fear in her eyes as they raced away from the attack.

Slocum had them rein up in a wash in the darkness. The hard-breathing horses blew and snorted, dancing around.

"Where can we go, Slocum?" Franco asked, riding in close. Maria leaned from behind him, her arms still tight around his waist, and with one hand she swept the hair from her face. "Our hacienda to the east. I know we would be safe there if my folks have not left for the wedding."

Slocum nodded. There would be few places in the desert to hide from Clanton's raiders when the sun came up. "We'll need to walk these horses a few miles," he said and booted the Morgan out. "Franco, you lead the way."

"We will," he said, and in the starlight Slocum saw the confident smile.

He dropped back and rode with Mary and the woman, Nita.

"Will they chase us?" Mary asked when he turned back from checking the back trail.

"No telling. They lost some men back there. I figure Clanton won't take his lack of success too well. He may put trackers on us. Sooner we are at this place the better."

The sun rose and they came into the land cultivated by the hacienda. Field workers, seeing and recognizing Maria riding behind Franco, removed their hats and chattered excited.

"See," she said back to Slocum. "There are many here."

These unarmed numbers did not count against Clanton's pistoleros, but he nodded and they rode on. The hacienda stood on the rise and looked like a castle with walls. They rode in and Slocum saw that there was no guard.

"Maria! Maria!" shouted a gray-haired woman all dressed to ride in the coach out front. She rushed out. "Oh, I am so sorry, we heard they murdered Don Leguna and we feared for your life."

"This is Franco and that is Slocum and Mary. They saved my life and saved Nita too."

"Such brave people. Get down, get down. My husband is gone to avenge their raid. We got word of the raid as we were getting up to go to the wedding."

"I hope Daddy will be careful."

"When they brought news of your fiancé's death, he left, afraid that you were dead or taken hostage also." Her mother rang her hands. "I am so sorry this could happen on your wedding day."

Maria shook her head and clung to Franco's arm. "Leguna

was in our camp when the raiders attacked. He ran past me like a coyote, with me crying for his help. He did not worry about me. Franco, he came and saved me—and his amigos, Slocum and Mary, they saved me and Nita."

Nita nodded. "Leguna only wished to save his own skin. These three are the ones."

"Why, señor?" Her mother looked pained at Slocum. "You wish a reward. My husband will pay you."

"No." He dropped his gaze. "Franco said we had to save her."

"Franco? Who are you? Why did you want to save her?"

"I love her." He patted the daughter's hand.

"Love her? How?" The señora looked aghast.

"I saw her on the road in that coach."

"But that is not love—"

"Only a man madly in love with a woman would have came back and fought like that," Slocum said.

"Or just mad." The woman told them to leave their horses; the help would take care of them. "Come inside. All of you. Her father should return, and maybe he can figure a way to repay you. You can't have my daughter, no matter how brave you are."

"Why can't he?" Slocum asked.

"Why . . . why, you can tell he is . . . nobody. Maria is heir to all of this. He could never manage this."

"But a coward who ran and left her in harm's way could have? Or did the fact he was a rancher's son make him better?"

"Better yes. Leguna knew . . ." She raised her chin and shook her head.

"Knew to save his back side and not her life?" Slocum asked.

"Did I say I was ungrateful? Maria, go to your room."

"No, Mother."

"Maria!" Her eyes slitted and her elbows jutted off her narrow waist.

"I am not a child. I learned a lot last night. When the man you promised would take such good care of me ran away."

"All right, I misjudged him. But this boy is a peon." She moved to separate her daughter from him. The two women struggled.

"I will hold who I want to hold," Maria said and moved to protect him from her wrath.

"We will see when your father returns."

"Yes, we will see," Maria said and led Franco toward the house. "Come, we should eat. My father will listen to reason."

Slocum shared a nod with Mary, and they came after the others.

"This looks like a castle in Europe," Mary said when they entered the two-story living room under the great chandelier. "I have seen paintings of them."

"This is only one of them."

"One?" She put her hand to her throat. "They have more?"

Slocum nodded. "Several other great ranches with homes as nice as this."

"How will Franco fare?" she asked under her breath.

"I think he has a damn good chance. A while ago I would never have guessed it. She may get over being grateful, but she's a forceful young woman on her own."

"Yes, I agree, and she truly felt abandoned last night."

"Oh, she'd never have married Leguna had he lived after he left her and Nita to those wolves."

"You said they tried to rape Nita?"

"One of them was raping her. I think she led him away from the coach to save Maria. She's very loyal, and the only reason I even found Maria or she ever agreed to come with me were Nita's words to the girl."

"What will her father say when he gets here?"

"I don't know him."

Mary grinned. "I thought you knew everyone in Mexico."

"Ah, only half."

"Come, señor, and you, señorita, and eat. While my daughter and I have such bad manners we argue in public—I am ashamed we act so poorly, for you have saved her."

"Sometimes things are trying," Slocum said, and escorted Mary to the long dining table.

Don Peralta and crew arrived with worn-out horses; their heads in the dust, coughing and snorting at sundown. The don dismounted and turned to see his daughter in the doorway, attached to Franco's arm.

Slocum had already begun to consider how Franco would have to ride on with only memories of this day, the time when an angel clung to him for hours and he stood at heaven's doorway with her. Heady business for a boy his age—Slocum knew. And Franco could look hard all his life in the face of every female he crawled into bed with, to see if it was her—then, when he learned the truth, look away and screw her ass off.

"Maria. My baby!" Peralta shouted at the sight of her. He rushed over and hugged them both. "I thought you were dead. Men, she is fine."

"Father, this is Franco."

"Nice to meet you, sir."

"He and Señor Slocum and Mary along with Nita saved me last night."

'I am sorry but . . . Leguna . . .'

"Father, he ran like a coyote with his tail between his legs and left me. Ran past me to save himself."

"Oh, no!" Don wailed and hugged the two of them.

"Father, I am going to marry Franco."

He stopped and blinked his eyes at her. "Has he asked you?"

"Yes, he has."

"And you said?"

"I would marry him."

"Then it will be, my child."

Slocum watched them kiss like starving pups and winked at Mary. "I'll be damned."

Maria Anita Consuela Peralta and Franco Consales were married five days later. After the elaborate ceremony, Slocum on Morgan and Mary on the dancing mare rode north with Uno carrying their provisions and bedding. Their at-arm's-length relationship continued. He didn't want to breach it without her consent, and she seemed happy. So they rode and camped under the stars each night. The final night they made camp up in the cooler junipers of the Muleshoes, at a stock tank watered by a spring.

"I may take a bath and wash my dress tonight," she said as the sun set and they sat on a log eating supper.

He nodded. "Last chance. We will be in Bowie tomorrow night."

"I know, and in ways I am sad. It has been very nice. You are a strong person. I have used your strength to recover since the first day you burst into that room."

"Apaches believe that if you kill a man you steal his strength."

She smiled. "I don't need to kill you. You were generous. You lent your strength to that boy too. If he had not ridden with you, he'd never have dared even speak to Maria, let alone steal her heart in that long ride."

"So?"

"So I will go back and teach school and find my place. But, Slocum, I will never again be afraid, for I have taken your strength and it is in my heart. What horrible things those two did to me are gone."

She began unbuttoning her dress. "You will excuse me now. I'll bathe and wash this dress."

"Yes, of course." He went off and smoked a cigarette. Squatted on the rimrock, he watched a blacktail buck make his way up the deep canyon in the twilight, flicking his tail, then clamping it down and browsing as he went. Testing the air, he kept his velvet rack high and never knew that his moves in the dying day were taken in by a human. Slocum could feel her hands slipping from his.

A week later, on the Prescott square, Slocum sat on the bench outside Hines Mercantile and read the latest edition of the *Prescott Miner*:

> *Apache Bronco Chief Caliche Killed This Week by International Troops in the Sierra Madres.*
> *Combined forces of the U.S. and the Mexican armies surrounded the Apache and his band in a canyon deep in the bowels of the mountains. Army scouts were led by an Apache woman, Kee, to his stronghold.*

SLOCUM AND THE APACHE CAMPAIGN   187

Slocum dropped the paper down a little to see who had stopped. The man getting off the parked wagon in the street looked familiar from the back. More so the hard-eyed woman coming after him. It was Thorpe and his wife, Claudia. Slocum kept the newspaper up, as they appeared to be headed for the store's door beside where he sat on the bench.

When they went past, he stood up, drew his six-gun and then slipped in behind them. "Keep your hands high, Thorpe. I'm arresting you for gunrunning, kidnapping and several more offenses."

"You—I should have kilt you that day down there!" Her part-Indian eyes snapped with anger.

Slocum nodded to her. "Yes, I guess you should have. But since the jail is just across the street, I won't have to go too far with him this time, will I?" He stuck Thorpe's six-gun in his waistband and shoved him around toward the courthouse.

"You no-good sumbitch—"

"Oh, as religious as you are, ma'am, I can't believe you would cuss like that. Get going," Slocum said and laughed. He laughed all the way to the jail across the square.